MW00721378

The Margo Chronicles
Copyright 2022 by CJ MacKinnon
ISBN: 9780-0-9730616-9-7
Published by Sparrow House Collective
www.sparrowhousecollective.com
jehooge@shaw.ca

Cover design: Joyelle Komierowski

THE MARGO
CHRONICLES

CJ MACKINNON

To my man,
without whom
this adventure would
never have begun!

TABLE OF CONTENTS

CHAPTER ONE

Day 20 of Margo's Retirement: The Evacuation Order

Only twenty days after she had moved into their newly purchased home, Margo answered a knock on the door and received a notice that threatened to blow the doors off the dream she and Michael had made for their retirement. Along with all the residents of the eighty-four homes that made up Wannatoka Springs, they received a hand-delivered order to evacuate their home immediately. A forest fire, burning out of control, was making a steady advance towards their tiny community despite the attack from the ground and the air. Days of thick smoke and acrid skies had forewarned this event, but for Margo and Michael, who came from the coast, this would be the first time in their lives that they would be the recipients of such news.

Margo had just retired at the end of June. A high school English teacher, she had taught her last class, packed up her desk, donated her files and resources to the next teacher, and turned out the lights of her classroom for very the last time. Neither she nor Michael knew a soul in Wannatoka Springs, but they fell in love with the tiny community on a lake, beyond the reach of the development of the expanding cities of the Okanagan, on the west side of the Monashees. The highway to the community was broken up by a lake, which required a ferry ride to get to the other side.

Like many others, Margo and Michael were looking to escape from the city. Living in British Columbia cities close to the 49th parallel, from Vancouver to the Okanagan, had become unfordable for the average retiree. Real estate had shot up in the last ten years or so, to the point that the smallest wartime houses on postage-stamp lots in Vancouver were going for a million dollars. Michael and Margo had spent all their working lives in a city suburb and owned their modest home, but they couldn't see themselves retiring there. They had seen their city outgrow and absorb the surrounding farmland and orchards, replacing them with tracts of industrial operations, and urban densification. Increasingly the community they knew was winnowed, and transformed into a suburban feed where the new inhabitants had their work and social life in the city and came home to sleep or relax when they didn't want to go out. The neighbours became and remained strangers, and the downtown core was gutted - first falling into disrepute and then rebuilt into more condos, high-rises and mega-malls. Which, in turn, led to higher prices, more traffic, noise, pollution and an increase in the crime rate; where there are new opportunities, there are opportunists.

Margo and Michael's dream was to sell their

house in the city, and move to a quiet town in the interior of B.C., somewhere peaceful with a nice big backyard with enough room for their yellow lab, Chance, to roam, and for Margo to read in the shade of an apple tree and Michael to have a real garden. They wanted this dream home to be in a neighbourhood where you knew your neighbours and felt safe. Not only safe to walk around, but a safe distance away from expanding developments. They found what they were looking for in Wannatoka Springs, a community unlikely to be touched by expansion or an invasion of city dwellers, as it was isolated and more than two hours' drive from the big box stores that people in the city found essential to their survival.

Competition was out of control where Margo and Michael lived, with house sales lasting only days or weeks on the market, or going into multiple offers and selling for well over asking as soon as the listing hit the Internet. But in the general area they were targeting, they found a newly renovated rancher with a walk-out basement at a price they found unbelievably low by coastal standards, and they put in an offer sight unseen.

It wasn't until after their offer was accepted that they visited their new purchase and scouted out the community. Fortunately, they were not disappointed. The house was everything they wanted and the neighbourhood was as friendly as they imagined.

But what Margo and Michael didn't account for, was how life in a small community differed from what they experienced living in an urban center. And that it was they, not the people who inhabited it, who had to make the cultural adjustment. Not only that, but this would be the first year they would not have to go to work or be responsible to account for their time or activities to anyone but themselves. Along the way, encounters and opportunities would confront their own assumptions and biases and identities. The first surprise came as Margo answered the door just twenty days into her life as a new retiree.

Margo was unpacking and organizing her kitchen when front door bell rang out. The chiming bell startled her. This was the first time it announced a visitor at the door. Michael thought the chimes were charming. Sometimes he would 'accidentally' lean on the door bell when he opened the front door. When he did, he always said, "Sorry! Nobody at the door. Just me. But aren't those chimes sweet? They remind me of Gram 'n Gramps house. Just like their old clock - without the bongs for the hour." Margo thought the chimes were an ostentatious announcement for a humble bungalow in a rural village in the middle of nowhere. She reminded herself again to have Michael change out these chimes that played a tune for an ordinary single or double bell. She opened the door just as the chimes were finishing their cycle.

Standing on the deck was a young, burly, red-bearded man wearing a yellow jacket with high viz orange stripes and Carharts. He held a clipboard in his right hand and referred to it when he talked to her, as if reading off a script.

"Good afternoon, ma'am," he said.

This was not a good start to an introduction, Margo thought. She intensely disliked being called 'ma'am by younger people - especially young men.

Far from sounding respectful, it sounded patronizing. Margo felt like she had been instantly assessed and categorized as 'old' by a member of the millennial generation.

"I'm Kyle," he said matter of factly. "I'm the volunteer fire chief here and I am going house to house to inform residents of the evacuation order for this area. Everyone has until 9 p.m. this evening to evacuate their homes. A temporary shelter has been set up in the James Douglas Arena in Crystal Lake. All residents are advised to pack up essential travel items, medications and any pets they might have and expect to vacate their homes for the duration of the order. Residents will not be allowed back into the area or their homes after they have evacuated for security and safety reasons. We will be setting up structural support including water suppression around the perimeter of the residential area so it is not necessary for individual home-owners to set up their own sprinkling systems to protect their individual dwellings. Do you have any questions, ma'am?"

"What?" was all Margo could supply as a response. She stared blankly at the young man, stunned by the news and struggled to form in her mind what this meant for her and her husband.

Kyle assumed he was either talking to an older deaf woman or an older daft woman, and so was ready to repeat his speech in a louder voice and at slower pace if necessary. He asked if there was anyone else in the house, thinking someone younger, maybe, could take charge and help this older woman get a grip on the situation.

"Is there anyone else living in this house, ma'am?

Husband? Children?"

The word 'ma'am' jolted Margo back to reality like a static electric shock jumping from a finger to her shoulder. She winced and drew herself up to meet his eye.

"My husband, Michael, is also a resident here," she said, looking down at the clipboard, noting that Kyle was a south paw. He was writing down the street number of their house. "And my name is Margo - not "Ma'am"." He looked up and cracked a small smile. Margo continued, "We have no children." She looked down again as Kyle started to write her first name. "Margo Gaetor. My husband's name is Michael - Michael Gaetor," she continued. Seeing that Kyle was hesitating after he had written down Michael's name, she offered, "Gaetor is spelled with an 'ae' "not like the abbreviation of the reptile." Margo had a lot of practice with spelling Michael's last name since she had taken it, and was fond of using this joke to break the ice and help people remember it.

"Can you spell that for me please, ma'am . . . sorry. Margo?" Kyle asked. He wasn't sure how 'gator' was spelled in the first place.

When they had completed the exchange and Kyle had written down their names, he looked up and said with a serious expression on his face, "OK. I think that wraps things up. Remember 9 p.m. You should download the app for B.C. wildfires, to get updates." He hesitated as if deciding whether to say something more while he looked at Margo, then said, "Are you familiar with what apps are? Or do you have a cell phone?"

"Yes. Michael and I both have one. Thank you. I'm

sure we can manage to download the app." Margo replied. *Ageism*! she thought. Who did these young people think they were talking to? She had managed to navigate the internet since the nineties and had one of the first cellphones offered by Blackberry. She probably had a cell phone in her hand while he was still sucking his thumb.

"Stay safe!" Kyle tucked his clipboard under his arm and walked back down their brick pathway to the street, where he continued on to the next house. Margo leaned on the open door watching him retreat. Her mind was whirling with what she ought to do next. How does one prepare for an evacuation? She blew out a breath, turned to go back in, and accidentally set off the door chime. It went through the rotation of notes like that old-fashioned clock Michael's grandparents had. Margo squeezed her eyes shut and rubbed her forehead.

"Michael!" She called out. "Michael! Stop what you're doing! Drop everything! We have an emergency."

CHAPTER TWO

Evacuation Essentials: Margo's List

What do you pack when you are told you have six hours to evacuate your home due to a wildfire roaring dangerously close to your community? Margo was tempted to search out a YouTube video to guide her though the process. Making a mental list, she went through the house, calling for her husband, Michael.

She found him in the backyard weeding the garden. Margo ran towards Michael waving frantically. "Michael!" she called, "Put down that hoe! We have an emergency!" Michael had been married to Margo for twenty-one years. He had seen her panic before. Sometimes she panicked over small things that could easily be fixed or taken care of like the water in the toilet draining sluggishly. Sometimes she panicked over invisible things like the time she was sure she heard a mouse in the wall behind the kitchen sink. It was an emergency! It had to be caught before she would step into the kitchen again to do another dish. Michael had set a trap. The trap sat beneath the sink for a week. Nothing. Still, Margo refused to go near the sink until Michael practically tore out the drainpipe and inspected every inch of the kitchen including the backs of every cupboard and behind the stove and fridge looking for rodent activity. Finding none, Michael assured Margo that there was no sign of any rodents in her immaculate kitchen. He was sure, if there had been a transient visitor, it had long moved on to more inviting quarters. Margo calmed down after Michael had made a thorough inspection and gave her the all clear.

Michael always accommodated Margo's panic attacks that way. He had learned there was no point in trying to ignore Margo or reason with her in these moments. That only escalated the behaviour. It fell to him to calm her down, first by taking her seriously, by investigating, and then diffusing the situation that caused her panic.

Michael looked up and saw his frazzled wife running across the grass towards him. With arms flailing and nearly tripping on an unseen clump of grass, she made her way to him shouting about an emergency. He leaned on his hoe trying to make out what Margo was going on about. In contrast to Margo's urgency, Michael stoically walked with his hoe, through the garden gate and waited for her to reach him so he could calm her down enough to allow her to tell him what she was panicking about.

"The fire chief was just here. Kyle - I think his name was. Young, stocky, bushy beard - you know the kind of facial hair millennial men like to grow. High-viz vest. Official looking. Anyway, he - Kyle, the fire chief told me . . ." She drew in a deep breath and continued. "That we are being evacuated because there's a wildfire burning its way towards us!" Margo stopped and looked at Michael's reaction. He raised his eyebrows and looked up at the forested hillside behind them, following the direction of Margo's arm.

"EVACUATION!" Margo repeated loudly, almost screeching. "Michael? Did you hear what I said?"

"Yes, I heard you. Evacuation. I half expected that," Michael countered calmly. "To say it's been pretty smoky these last two weeks would be an understatement. The smoke is choking out here. When did he say we had to be out of here?" Michael leaned his hoe on the fence and started taking off his gardening gloves.

"When?" Margo was still panicked. "Now! That's when! By 9 p.m. he said! Michael! It's an evacuation order! We might lose our home! Why are you so non-chalant about this? You're acting as if I just called you to come in for dinner?"

Michael stepped closer to his wife. "Because, my love, it won't help to get worked up about it." He put an arm around her waist and drew her close to him. "We have to think about what to do next. And to think about that clearly, we have to put out of our heads what might or might not happen. From what you have explained, we have approximately six hours to pack up our belongings. We need to gather up our essential papers and whatever we think is valuable to us. We will also need to pack clothes and personal toiletries we will need for the trip. And we'll need to pack up dog food and whatnot for Chance, and get his kennel from the basement. He may need to be boarded. Then we have to pack up our car and get out of here by nine if not before. Now what were Kyle's instructions exactly?"

Margo listened to Michael's litany of things to take care of. Hearing his rational voice helped her calm down. As they walked towards the house, she repeated Kyle's message and explanation about what to do. Michael stopped at the garden shed to hang up his hoe, still listening to Margo. When she had finished, he said calmly, "You go in and start packing like Kyle said, clothes and things you think you will need to get you through three or four days. Then look for essential papers like our insurance contract, the title to the house, our birth certificates and passports - anything we might need to show to the authorities should the worst-case scenario occur. After you complete that task, gather up the things you value that can't be replaced - like photographs. I'll join you soon. I want to do some things out here to protect our house in case there is a fire. And Margo," he looked at her straight in the eye and held her arms gently, "it's going to be OK. We're going to be OK. We have insurance. We have means. We have each other - and Chance."

Chance, a golden lab cross was sitting calmly beside Michael while he talked to Margo. He looked up when Michael mentioned his name. Michael scratched his ear. When Margo erupted into the backyard shouting for Michael, Chance had been snoozing under the plum tree. He shook off his sleep and sat up abruptly when he heard Margo's voice. He walked over to where the couple was talking, but took his cue from Michael and had not reacted to Margo's panicked voice.

Michael's tone and assurances soothed Margo and she began to breathe easier, regaining control of her emotions. When she wasn't in a panic, Margo was quite capable of thinking strategically. She stepped inside the house as Michael disappeared into the garden shed. Chance sat in the yard at the spot where the two had parted ways, panting and smiling. After a moment's hesitation, he decided to follow Michael around the yard.

For the next two hours Margo furiously packed, repacked, exchanged and rearranged what she thought she wanted to preserve in the event of a fire. She had first sat down and made a list, but as one thing was found and struck off invariably another appeared. The list didn't seem to get any longer or shorter, but the pile beside the door was growing.

She reasoned with herself about how to prioritize personal items and memorabilia. How far should she go back? Should she include the scrapbook she had made in elementary school? Yes. It was a memento from her past that she had hung onto all these years and could never replace. Then there was her mother's Royal Doulton china. She had fought her sisters for it when her mother passed away, but rarely used it. No. The set was a nostalgic keepsake, but not really useful and not irreplaceable. Besides it would probably get broken in the car.

Then there was the VHS tape of her first wedding. It has been thirty years ago. The marriage lasted only seven years but the videotape captured one of the proudest moments of Margo's life. She had taken a minor in theatre in college, and hoped one day she would become a playwright and a theatre director. The man she was engaged to aspired to be an actor. Marriage seemed to be a natural fit for two fledgling theatre aspirants. Instead of making their way on their own, they could lean on each other for support and financial constancy. They would move to New York. One could work while the other found a role in a theatre production. Then they would switch. The one who had a run in a play would find some insignificant job, like waiting on tables, so the other could take their turn to be discovered.

They had big dreams. Margo's was of writing and directing plays that would be produced in professional theatre - off Broadway, and then on Broadway someday. Her fiancé dreamed of acting. The play's the thing that brought them together. Margo had even choreographed and staged their wedding as a pageant. Everyone in the wedding party was actors and singers - and everyone played a role.

The marriage, though, didn't turn into a happily ever after ending as the pageant promised it to be. The pair didn't make it to New York - or even into professional theatre. After a few trial runs in community theatre and no calls to ply their talents on the professional stage, their aspirations began to wane and the pressing matter of staying afloat financially took precedence over their dreams. Margo's major at college was in English. When their marriage, along with their dreams, dissolved, Margo went back to university to complete her teacher's degree. She had been a teacher ever since. The VHS tape of her wedding pageant was all she had left to remind her of those dreams. She kept it in a box with her wedding album long after DVDs replaced VCRs and even after

DVDs were replaced by live streaming. She looked at it now and sighed. Tentatively she tossed it back in the box. Not everything from the past could be salvaged.

Margo went through other mementos she had saved over the years: projects and stories that her students had done, gifts her students had given her over the years, the books she had collected, letters she had held onto from her parents and friends, the clothing and costume jewelery she had collected and worn during her teaching career, and other personal items she held sentimental.

When she had exhausted her list of priorities, and had gone through the pile she had made of 'must keep items' she went through them again to pare them down, realizing there wouldn't be room in their car to take everything she had collected over the years. She put them into two piles: the 'must take' and the 'if there's room' piles. Margo was standing near the front door trying to think of anything she had missed when Michael called from the back door.

"Margo! Come out here! I want to show you something!"

Margo was so absorbed in her own world of decision-making that she hadn't noticed the time. It didn't register until she heard his voice that Michael had not been in the house looking for his own treasures. Margo descended the stairs and walked toward the back door.

"Michael, do you know what time it is? What have you been doing? We only have two hours left!"

"I know." Michael said, "I've been busy preparing for the protection of our house in the event of a fire. Come and look." He held the door open for Margo to walk out into the backyard first and then guided her towards the side of the house. When they turned the corner, Margo saw a network of garden hoses that crisscrossed each other, draped over the balcony to the deck above them and curled up and over the rose bush at the front corner of the house. A sprinkler dangled from the end of one hose wound around the roses. Another was sitting on the railing of the deck attached to the hose that was draped over it. And a third was at the end of a hose that had been extended on the ground to about ten meters away from the house. To Margo it looked like the snaking tendrils of Hydra!

"What's all this?" she asked, hands on hips.

"Fire protection." Michael acted with almost gleeful energy as he hopped through the labyrinth of hoses on the ground, and made his way to the outdoor tap, which had been fitted with a manifold with hose hook-ups that could distribute water through a nest of hoses, to all points of the compass.

"Stand over there!" Michael waved his hand behind him. Margo stepped backward into the yard about five meters. "Watch this!" He twisted the tap counter-clockwise. Margo heard the water hiss and the sprinklers spit. After about thirty seconds all of the sprinklers spurted out water. The side of the house, including the upper deck was soaked in a matter of minutes.

Michael ran out from under the deck where he was standing and stood with Margo admiring his handiwork. "Don't you worry, Margo, with this system all the ground crew have to do is turn on the tap. Our house will be the last one to burn if it comes to that."

Margo was secretly proud of Michael for looking after the safety of their home but at the same time she was annoyed at him for using up so much precious time.

"That's all well and good, Michael. But the ground crew and security detail are laying hoses right down the street that will be accessible to a fire hydrant. I think you should make packing up and preparing to leave our home your priority.

Michael sighed and ducked under the water streaming down the deck to turn off the hoses. "Margo," he muttered under his breath, as he went, "just doesn't understand what the real priorities are."

By 7 p.m. Michael had packed his belongings and stacked them next to Margo. He studied Margo's two piles. "What is this?" he asked.

"The one closest to the door is the 'must go' pile and the other one is the 'not unless there is room' pile."

Michael shrugged, "OK but you know we have a big dog in a big crate that will take up a lot of the back seat. So you might have to cull that 'must go' pile a little more. But for you, I'll do my best."

Michael was the most careful, strategic packer Margo knew. She felt confident he would find room for as much of what she wanted to go with them as he could shift, slide, shimmy, and stuff into every available cranny of their vehicle.

"Not much room left," Michael said. He had packed both of their suitcases, their electronics tote bags, the dog crate and all the essentials they would require if they had to overnight in a facility set up for emergencies "But if we are careful we can get most of your 'must go' items in." Michael smiled and winked at Margo as he passed her, her arms full of personal mementos she had carefully wrapped and packed. She winced.

There was actually quite a bit of room. His suitcase was much smaller and lighter than Margo's so there was room in the trunk. Chance's crate took up half the back seat, but their electronics totes fit into the back seat foot-wells, so the other half was still waiting to be filled.

Margo started pushing what was in her arms into the sides of the trunk.

"What are you bringing?" Michael asked astonished.

"I thought I should bring an extra coat and a pair of boots in case the weather turned cold." It was forty degrees Celsius and not a cloud in the sky.

Michael shook his head. "It will be a cold day in hell before that happens."

"So you don't think I should take them?"

And so it went for the next hour, Margo hauling out items in her 'yes' pile and Michael questioning the validity of taking them. Tempers began to rise to the heights of the temperature outside before they had finished. But the strategic packer and the not-so-strategic decision-maker finally came to terms with what could and could not fit into their vehicle and by 8:30 p.m.

Michael was making his rounds around the house to make sure the doors and windows were secured and that the lights were all turned off while Margo fussed with Chance to coax him into his crate. Chance sized up his destination and immediately started a game of 'catch me if you can' with Margo running around the car after him cursing and threatening him until he decided he had to surrender or die. Margo had gotten Chance settled just as Michael came out of the house, locked the door and walked down the sidewalk to the vehicle. They were off on their new adventure.

"Are you sure you remembered everything?" Michael asked as he was buckling his seatbelt.

"I think so," Margo replied, but then undid her seatbelt. "Oh, wait. I think there is something I forgot." With that, she opened the car door, leapt out, and ran toward the house. Michael looked at his watch. Precisely two minutes and thirty seconds later, Margo emerged carrying over her shoulder what looked like a bulging pillowcase. She looked to Michael as if she were a burglar furtively making a get away with her loot.

"Hey!" he said, leaning out the open driver's side window, "What's in the sack?"

"Just a few personal things I just couldn't leave behind." Margo said, raising her head and daring her to question him. "I saw there was a little room in the trunk. I'm sure this will fit."

Michael rolled his eyes. He loved his wife, but he wasn't above playing tit for tat with her. He jerked the driver's side door open and stalked into the house as Margo was stuffing the contents of her pillowcase into the trunk.

"Where are you going? I thought you said we were ready to go."

Michael waved with the back of his hand, "Just forgot something. I'll be right there."

When he re-emerged from the house, Michael was carrying a pillow case over one shoulder. Margo looked at him annoyed, but stopped herself from saying anything. In silence, he opened the trunk. Margo felt the suspension on the vehicle ride up and down with Michael's struggle to rearranged some things, and cram his bulky pillowcase into a space, and then felt the trunk slam shut.

Michael took up his seat, buckled his seatbelt and turned the engine on. "And we are off. Let's get this Evac-ation started!"

Margo didn't share Michael's optimism, and looked wistfully through the side mirror as their house disappeared around the block. She hoped she would see it again and that it would be intact, but mentally she was preparing herself for the worst.

Michael waved to the volunteer fire brigade and security crew guarding the entrance to the community and directing traffic one way - out. No one except the fire crew would be allowed to enter until the order was lifted.

After a kilometer or two, Margo blew out a long breath. This was actually happening! In the dark, beside her she heard, 'Snap! Pop! Fizz'. She recognized the sound. Margo looked over at Michael. He was steering with his left hand while holding a beer in his right.

"What are you doing, Michael?" Margo hissed, and looked surreptitiously in her passenger side mirror.

"Having a beer to calm my nerves," Michael said and smiled sideways at Margo. "Want one?"

"No!" she said emphatically. "What do you

mean? You never do that! What are you going to say if a cop pulls you over?" She looked into the mirror again to see what was behind them.

"I'll say, Officer, I beg your pardon. This is the first time I have ever done this. It is also the first time we have had to evacuate due to the threat of a wildfire consuming our home and all of our possessions. We have no idea where we are going to lay our heads tonight or if we will have a home to come home to when this is all over. So please . . . just this once . . . let this lawless behaviour slide and I swear I will never commit another offence again." Michael finished his declaration with another sip of beer and punctuated it with a belch.

Margo giggled - both because she was nervous and because she was seeing a side of Michael she hadn't seen before. A playful, reputation-be-damned recklessness. She would grow to like that, she thought.

The smoke was so thick they couldn't see what was in front or behind them except for the blurry red flashes of break lights that indicated they were in a parade of evacuees travelling away from the security of their homes toward an uncertain destination.

Margo watched bits of ash steadily falling onto the windshield like snowflakes as they drove down the highway. She peered into the eerie greyness of the not-yet-dark summer night shrouded in smoke from the nearby fire.

"Is it Armageddon yet?" she asked.

Michael used to ask Margo that question in mock horror when she came to him like Chicken Little, hysterical about some calamity she foresaw raining down on them.

Now here they were. In the midst of a real calamity that may just rain down fire. And here they were, laughing at their inside joke.

If you're curious about what Margo and Michael brought out of the house in those last-minute grab bags, here's a list of what they thought they couldn't leave behind.

Michael's inventory of must haves:
- An autographed paperback copy of *Roadside Attraction* a novel signed by his favourite author, Tom Robbins himself, who he met once.
- Two binders of songs he had written over the years, mostly hand-copied originals, and the only ones in existence.
- His mother's Bible.
- His dad's junior hockey commemorative plaque.
- About 100 or so hockey cards from his collection - going back to Bobby Orr and Mario Lemieux as well as his prize Wayne Gretzky rookie card. It was in mint condition.
- His deceased dog's ashes still held in a coffee container. He hadn't been able to scatter them yet.
- A knitted teddy bear made by his mother before he was born.
- A six-pack of beer. Five others were stashed behind the driver's seat.

Margo's inventory of must haves:
- A plaque she always kept on her desk - a quote by Ralph Waldo Emerson, which read, "Once you make a decision, the universe conspires to make it happen."
- Her mother's set of wedding silverware (the china would have been too fragile but the silverware would

remind her of their special family dinners - and might be worth something if they needed to cash it in someday.

- Three more pairs of shoes and a pair of boots, just in case. And a heavy jacket. You never knew when it was going to snow in Canada.

- Five paperback novels she had just picked up at the thrift store the week before for fifty cents apiece. She intended to read them this summer. If it was going to be a long evacuation she might need some reading material. In her panic, she failed to reason that she could store ten times that number on her electronic reader that was already packed in her electronics tote.

- A funny birthday card Michael gave her one year that had a picture taken from the rear of a plump Eastern European peasant woman dressed in a traditional flowered cotton dress with a scarf tied over her hair, sitting on a donkey. The caption read, "Does this dress make my ass look big?"

- The VHS tape of her first wedding. It was irreplaceable after all, she reasoned, even though she knew she would   never play it. She recycled her VCR long ago.

CHAPTER THREE

Backseat Driver

"Hop in!" Michael shouted to Margo over the sound of ATV motor. The Arctic Cat side-by-side came with the purchase of their house. The previous owner was so excited that someone actually made an offer on the house he had put on the market five years ago, he offered to throw his ATV into the deal if they met his asking price.

The asking price was the same price the owner listed it for five years ago. He had stubbornly hung onto that price believing his house was worth every penny since he had made significant renovations and honestly felt that it was the best house in Wannatoka Springs. Five years before, his asking price was more in line with the housing market on the coast, but in this area it was outrageous, especially as it was located in a community with no services except a self-service gas pump and a postal outlet and it was too far away from any city or town to be considered within a commutable distance for work.

However, Wannatoka Springs was a community

waiting to be discovered. In five years the prices of houses on the coast and in other major cities in Canada had doubled. And the same five years saw more baby boomers vacating the workforce and finding they could live anywhere for less than in the city. Many house-rich boomers who were on a fixed income, sold while prices peaked on the coast and bought at much more reasonable prices in the interior. The migration began to trickle and then pour into the towns and villages established to accommodate the silver mining industry in the late 19th Century.

Since the inexpensive extraction of resource had been exhausted, the villages were abandoned as people moved on to brighter prospects, leaving those who made their living on farms or in the forests in the sparsely populated area. The Kootenays, a nearly hidden pocket in the lower part of the province, was discovered once before in the late 60's and early 70's as a haven for dreamers and dodgers who wanted to cut themselves off from the establishment and homestead. The hippies and loggers co-existed for decades, but neither predicted the encroachment on what they both considered their land. But as folks abandoned homestead living and moved back to where there was work - or retired from the trades and moved to more convenient locations that had medical services, and closer to their children, a gap opened up once again and a whole new wave of dreamers and dodgers seeking to get away, swept in.

Relatively young, healthy retirees who had capital to invest, and some disposable income to spend, found themselves traveling through these small, historic towns and villages woven through a fabric of lakes and mountains and trees in the Columbia Basin. The villages and homes might be a little shabby and unfashionable, but they were delightfully affordable. The most ambitious could see the potential with a little upgrade here and there. The least ambitious found their level of habitation and were content just to have found a place less competitive and judgmental.

The house Margo and Michael fell in love with in Wannatoka Springs (a name they had never heard before) came in at what they considered a bargain price! And an ATV thrown in with the asking price was almost an unfair bargain, Michael thought. Having grown up in the city, he had never driven one before. But he imagined it would be a great adventure to comb the mountainsides for wood, and drive it on off-road expeditions. How hard could it be? Just a little more than a riding lawnmower.

Margo had no interest whatsoever in driving the thing. Anything to do with forest adventures where there were no signs to lead her back to civilization, or towards a possible bear citing, made her anxious. She couldn't imagine driving an all terrain vehicle all over the countryside or in the woods just for fun. But Michael seemed excited about the offer. An ATV would be practical, he argued. He could use it to haul wood for the wood stove - or haul away branches from pruned trees. And maybe because it was a side-by-side (which meant two seats in the front and a box in the back) he and Margo could even take it to a remote beach to have a picnic.

Margo was not impressed with any of Michael's ideas. To her, that contraption, as she called it, was a death wish waiting for a senior to make it happen. But she didn't think it was worth an argument. The thought of owning one made Michael happy. Besides, everyone in the neighbourhood seemed to have some sort of ATV parked in their driveway. She had even seen them being driven down the street when they had first visited their home and new town. If possessing one excited Michael about tasks he could see himself doing in his retirement and helped him see himself fitting in to his new neighbourhood, who was she to cloud his visions.

Before the evacuation, Michael had taken the ATV out a few times on the logging road that led out of the community and into the bush to test it. Actually he was testing himself. He was nervous about driving it, but was determined to learn how on his own. He didn't want to ask for help from one of the local men who he could see handling theirs with ease because that might make him look naive - which he was, of course, but he didn't want it to be the first impression. At first it lurched and bucked in mild protest like a horse that wasn't used to being ridden by inexperienced riders. After a few false starts and jerky stops, Michael got the hang of it.

One fine morning, Michael suggested to Margo they take a ride with their dog, Chance, down to the beach. They could ride along the shore and let Chance out to swim or fetch sticks in the water. Margo sighed. She wanted to resist but she could see how much pride Michael took in honing his driving skills. She agreed as long as Chance could be safely transported in the short box behind the seats. Michael assured her that he could rig up a harness of some sort that would ensure Chance's safety.

On the morning of their first ATV adventure to the beach, Michael rolled up to the front lawn to fetch Chance. He wanted to settle the nervous passenger one at a time.

Chance sat in the backyard watching Michael maneuver the vehicle through the gate and onto the front lawn. He cocked his head to one side, and then to the other, panting all the while. It was a warm, sunny day with almost no breeze. A good day for a swim. On other days like this Margo had walked him down to the beach, but had kept him on a long rope and allowed him to paddle out into the lake until the rope became taut, then Chance would swim back. Chance, a city-bred dog, had, up to now, lived a sheltered life: on-leash walks on city streets, frisbee catch in off-leash dog parks. Like Michael, he had his fantasies about getting out to explore the new wilderness landscape his people had moved him to, but as he sat there watching Michael tie ropes in loops onto the sides of the strange, noisy, highly suspicious machine, he had no clue how close he was going to come to hearing the call of the wild on this warm summery day.

"Chance! Come here boy!" Michael coaxed, holding Chance's leash out for him to see. Someone holding his leash meant he would get to go for a walk and Chance was always up for going for a walk. It was mostly Margo who walked him though, and it was Margo who had trained him. So, although he liked Michael's company and particularly sought out his company when Margo was in panic mode, he sided with her. When Michael tried to command him to do something, he thought of it as optional - a suggestion he could take or leave. Michael often had to resort to food bribery to get Chance to do what he wanted. If that failed, Michael gave the problem child over to Margo with a comment like, "He's YOUR dog! You deal with him."

Today it was important for Michael that he show

Margo he was in charge - to gain her confidence. He knew she would be nervous and didn't want Chance to add to her worries. When Chance walked towards the leash, tail wagging, Michael stretched out his hand in a fist. Chance smelled something he liked and licked the closed fist while Michael hooked the leash to his collar. That done, Michael opened his hand and let Chance take the tasty morsel he brought with him. So far so good, Michael thought, as he walked the dog through the gate, closed it, and walked toward the side-by. Chance was pulling on his leash excitedly as they approached the road, because he thought they were going for a walk around the block where a mixture of smells and sights attracted his attention and prompted him to leave his mark. But when Michael stopped at the rear of the vehicle, stiffening his hold on the leash, Chance became wary. He stopped in his tracks and would not budge when Michael stood with him at the tailgate urging him to jump up into the box in front of him. Michael slackened his grip on Chance's leash and patted the floor of the box with his free hand saying, "Jump up boy! C'mon! Jump! In! You and I and Margo are going to take a ride to the beach!"

All Chance heard was "Jump! Blah, blah, Jump! Blah, blah, blah, Margo, blah, blah, blah, Beach!" He pulled again on his leash but this time in the opposite direction. He backed up, trying to pull Michael away as if he were dragging him away from a dangerous situation. Michael was not deterred. He knew Chance might take some persuading. He reached into his pocket and pulled out another treat. "It's OK Chance. No one is going to hurt you. Look. I have something nice for you. And then we are going to take you for a ride. Won't that be a treat?" Chance heard, "Chance.

33

Blah, blah, blah. Look. Blah, blah, blah and then treat?" He stretched his neck out far enough to lick up the treat in Michael's hand while keeping the rest of his body out of range.

Michael is one of those dog owners who think they can reason with their dog like they are small children. He thought if you explained everything to them and it made sense, they would cooperate more willingly. He never accepted that dogs have selective hearing. Nor did he understand that an adult dog is not like a small child. You can't fool an old dog into doing new tricks like you can a kid, with the promise of a treat. You have to have the treat in your hand to even negotiate with an adult dog. Promising a treat at some unforeseeable and intangible time in exchange for cooperation now, fell on unbelieving and uncooperative ears.

Michael moved closer to Chance, drawing in the length of the leash as he went, and talking to the dog in a singsong voice he hoped was soothing if not understandable. When close enough, he slipped his hand under Chance's collar and pulled him as gently as he could pull a eighty pound dog who was digging all fours into the ground toward the back of the side-by. Slowly Michael gained ground. Inches away from the back bumper, Michael swooped down and enclosed Chance in an embrace around his tummy. With a grunt, Michael lifted and pushed the dog's dead weight up and into the box. First the dog's front leg's and the front half of his body, and then, with a shove at the rear, his back end. Once Chance was in the box, Michael hopped up with him and, still talking to him in a singsong voice, strapped on the harness he had made by tying together thick ropes that wouldn't cut or hurt Chance if he moved. Chance tried to wriggle out of the harness Michael fitted around his chest, but Michael managed to secured it with the two ropes tied to either side of the box. Michael made one last test of its durability by leaning back himself against the side ropes that were hooked onto Chance's harness. Chance didn't have a chance of escape.

With one nervous passenger secured, he called Margo out. She was less stubborn and at least he didn't have to lift her into her seat, but she didn't listen to Michael's encouragement or instructions either. Finally he came around to her side, buckled the seat strap where it should be and put her hand onto the roll bar so she knew where she could grab to steady herself if she was nervous. Having done that, he snapped the safety net by Margo's feet closed and swung into the driver's seat. Michael was sweating by the time they left the yard, not because it was a warm day but because he had already exerted so much effort and their adventure had not yet begun. Michael gripped the wheel and whistled a little tune as he pushed the gas pedal down smoothly. Margo clutched the roll bar (even though they were driving down a paved road) and ground her teeth. Chance swayed from side to side in his harness in the back, and panted. He wasn't smiling.

When they reached the beach, Michael navigated over the rocky and uneven terrain parallel to the shoreline, with caution. He was never an over-driver and didn't want Margo's first experience in the ATV to be upsetting. After a while, Margo found her rhythm and loosened her grip on bar. The wind blowing through her hair and the sunshine beating down on her head through the open frame made her feel something she hadn't felt in a long time. Something like what she felt when she was a child, playing on her cousin's farm. It had been so long since she felt carefree that she couldn't find the word to describe it right away. Carefree! That was the word for it! Margo raised her arms above her head, stretched her face up to the sunshine, and let out a long, loud bout of carefree laughter.

"Woohoo!" Margo cried when they were driving through a shallow bog. "Ride 'em cowboy!" She swung her free arm around above her head like she was swinging a lasso while holding on tight to the roll bar with the other as she swayed back and forth with the dips and bumps along their path. Michael straddled the uneven beach-front with the cocky swagger of a cowboy showing off his bronco riding skills to his girl. In the back, Chance swayed and skidded with every rut a tire struck and each mound the machine climbed over, first to one side and then the other, restrained from leaping over the side by the ropes that held him in. Margo looked back and saw the worried look on Chance's face. "Why don't we let Chance out for a run! I think he's ready to run free," Margo shouted over the loud motor.

"OK. Sure." Michael agreed, stopped the side-by on a grassy bar close to the water, and untied Chance's harness. As soon as he could feel he was free from the constraints, he leapt out of the vehicle, ran in circles around it, then bounded down the beach. He turned back once, charged Michael - as if to say, "Never again! You won't trick me ever again with the promise of a treat!" And then pulled up and spun around, running full-tilt down to the lake-shore. Margo and Michael laughed at Chance's antics; twists and turns, into the water and out again, up the hill and charging down it and then running further down the beach. They laughed and called out to egg him on. He looked so free and happy. They were joyful just watching him. They kept their eyes on Chance until he rounded a bend and they lost sight of him.

"Hmm . . . " Margo mused, shading her eyes as she looked down the beach where he had disappeared. "I wonder if he will come back. He's never really been free to just run." She worried however Chance might not know where he was going or when to come back. "Chance! Come!" Margo shouted, cupping her hands around her mouth to get more volume. She waited and scanned the beach. No response. She whistled. He didn't respond. Michael also tried to call. They shouted together. But Chance was nowhere in sight.

"Lets get in and chase him down," Margo said, as she climbed into her seat. Michael had the same thought at the same time. He was already climbing back into the driver's seat. Margo struggled with the awkward mount, having had little practice stepping up and swinging her body into the seat. When she managed to get herself in and belted she shouted, "I'm in! Let's go!' She gave Michael the thumbs-up and then grabbed the bar.

Maneuvering through the rocks, debris and logs, Michael gained ground yard by painstaking yard, of the beach in the direction Chance had run off. While Michael concentrated on not tipping over with one set of wheels suspended over the debris that the other set were grinding through, Margo let her thoughts run away with her. *What if Chance was stuck between two logs or his collar snagged by fallen branch? What if he swam too far out into the lake chasing a goose and the current took him away?* Crystal Lake is a reservoir not a river. There is no current. But that detail didn't stop Margo from conjuring up the image of her poor Chance helplessly bobbing down a rapid with a goose flapping in his jaws. *What if a wild animal attacked him?* Margo shut down her tunnel of doom and focused on the space around them, fearing the worst but willing herself not to give in to it just yet.

Never did it cross Margo's mind that Chance was just enjoying his newfound freedom. As it turned out, Chance was elated to find an unobstructed stretch of land to run around on - and a myriad of scented trails to follow. He forgot he was an obedient, suburban, city dog, and felt for a moment instinctively wild and free.

"We'll never catch Chance at this speed, Michael!" Margo shouted. "Step on it!" Michael was surprised to hear Margo's urgent request for more speed. She was usually telling him he was going too fast or not watching the road closely enough. But with his new intoxication came a sense of power and immortality and so he didn't hesitate to press his foot down on the accelerator.

"To the floor!" he shouted back to Margo. The ATV lurched into high gear. The top speed was about 50 kilometers per hour, but on this terrain Michael held it back to 30. Still it felt to Margo that they were flying. She hung onto the bar for dear life, swaying with every uneven roll of the tires. Michael bent over the steering wheel concentrating on maneuvering the vehicle, avoiding the larger rocks. Both looked ahead and to the side searching for signs of their dog.

They spotted Chance above them on the side of the

hill. He had pulled up short by a clump of bushes growing out of the rock and was concentrating on the message that was left there by another animal. Then he left a message of his own with a half-lifted leg. "There he is!" Margo shouted and pointed at the golden lab crouching beside the clump.

"I see him!" Michael shouted back. "Hold on, Margo. This is going to be a steep climb!" And he swerved the side-by toward the bank where Chance was standing now, placidly looking down on them. But Chance didn't like the sound of the encroaching vehicle. And perhaps he remembered standing in the back of it, unsure of his footing and swaying from side to side, unable to break free. Nimbly, he scrambled higher up the slope. Soon he found an animal path that he could easily navigate and sauntered down a short way.

"Chance!" Margo cried, cupping her hands around her mouth. "Chance! Come!" Usually hearing this command would bring her dog back immediately. But whether it was the wind, which had picked up, or the roar of the motor or an unwillingness to give up his newfound freedom, Chance did not respond.

"Hang on!" Michael shouted to Margo over the noise of the engine, "Let's see what this baby can do!" He coaxed the ATV slowly up and sideways in a zigzag fashion so it wouldn't lose its vertigo. Margo clenched her teeth and her thighs - and crossed her heart for good measure. She wasn't a praying person, but at this moment, she offered one up anyway. "Please God. Bring my Chance back and I'll never let him wander off again." She thought better of that promise later. But then most people who make promises when they are in dire straits do that when the trouble clears up and they find themselves alive and well.

When the path straightened out, Michael blew out a long whistle and Margo let out her breath. Until then, she didn't realize she was holding it. This was turning out to be the first sincerely exhilarating adventure she had had since she was a child. Ahead of them Chance was standing on the path, his nose buried at the base of a bush, reading another message. Michael stopped the ATV abruptly when he saw the dog. Margo rocked back and sucked in a breath.

"Wait here," she said, "I'll get him. He'll respond better to me if I'm walking and we're not chasing him down with this contraption."

It's an ATV not a contraption, Michael noted mentally. His girl might not be so impressed, but he was sure proud of himself. He had navigated up a rocky hillside and risked life and limb to save a headstrong dog that didn't want to be saved - all for the sake of his wife. That should count for something.

Margo walked slowly and as nonchalantly as she could towards Chance. She didn't want to startle him into a run again. "There you are, Chance," she said in a soothing voice. Chance continued to take in the fascinating smells at the base of the bush. "You gave me quite a scare," she said as she advanced slowly towards Chance. When she was close enough to touch him she grabbed his collar firmly with one hand and deftly clipped leash to it with the other.

"Come, Chance!" she commanded. And without hesitation, Chance snapped back into the obedient dog he was trained to be and trotted beside her, panting and smiling.

When the side-by was in sight, Chance stopped

abruptly, refusing to walk any closer. Margo tried to command him to come with her, and pulled at his leash to encourage him forward but he dug in his heels. There was no way he was getting into the back of that thing and tied up in that harness again.

Michael jumped out of the driver's seat. "Keep holding onto his leash Margo, but give it lots of slack!" he instructed. "I'll grab him!" Michael circled Chance's middle again, but this time Chance knew what his fate would be and struggled hard against him. He twisted free and shied away from Michael. Michael tried coaxing him by putting his front paws up on the open tailgate and then pushing his butt up from behind. Chance twisted around, flipped over Michaels shoulder and was down again on all fours, panting. Fairly warned about what Michael was trying to do, Chance backed away just out Michael's reach when he tried to approach him, and wound his leash around Margo's legs.

Exasperated, Michael shouted to Margo. "Call your damn dog! Either he gets in the vehicle or he'll be running along behind it with his leash tied to the hitch."

"No! You wouldn't! I mean you couldn't . . . " Margo replied. "Never mind. I don't want to know. Leave it to me. I'll get him in." Margo tried once more to coax Chance to hop in on his own, but he stubbornly stood his ground and would not move.

"Let's try this," Margo said to Michael in an uncharacteristic calm and rational voice. "I'll get in on the driver's side. You lead Chance around to the passenger side. He likes riding shotgun in the car when I take him out on drives. Maybe he'll sit in the passenger seat with me. And I can drive us home."

"What??" Now it was Michael who panicked. "You

can't drive this thing! It's a big machine! You said yourself it was a death trap for seniors. Why would you want to risk all three of our lives? And where would I sit? In the middle?"

Margo was already climbing into the driver's seat and strapping herself in with the seatbelt. "I can drive a car, can't I? And I've driven the lawn tractor haven't I? So I don't see why can't I drive this! And, no, you can't sit in the middle. There's no room. You'll have to sit in the back - in the box." Margo adjusted the mirror, waiting for Michael to lead Chance around to the open passenger side of the ATV.

Michael was flabbergasted. He was about to try to reason with Margo when Chance freed himself from his grip on the leash he let slacken, and jumped willingly into the passenger seat beside Margo. Eyes forward, Chance sat in the passenger seat panting and smiling.

"Dammit Margo! And damn your dog too!" Michael called out just as Margo, a little heavy- footed on the gas, brought the ATV to life with an unexpected roar. There was no use in objecting. Margo was in the driver's seat, Chance was the passenger, and Margo was securing Chance's leash to the back of the seat so he couldn't leap out.

Straining, Michael hoisted himself into the back and pulled up the tailgate behind him. The back wasn't really meant for passengers. It was a short metal box with a ridged floor and nothing to cushion his seat when he slumped down, his back against the back of the cab. "You better not tip this thing, Margo!" Michael shouted. "I don't have much to hang onto!"

"Don't worry! I'll be careful!" Margo called back to him. "Grab both ropes and hang on!" She turned around and flashed Michael a smile. Chance wasn't the only one enjoying the freedom of adventure.

Famous last words, Michael thought miserably. He grabbed the ropes on both sides, and braced himself for the ride. "OK. I'm ready." Michael called out. Ready for what? He didn't want to think about it so he fixed his eyes on the rear view, avoiding the temptation to look to see what was ahead.

"Hang on!" Margo said over her shoulder, and then yelled into the air, "Woohoo! Ride 'em cowgirl!" she said as she lurched forward unevenly, trying to get the hang of how hard to step on the gas and break pedals. Margo picked her way forward along the path that Chance had led them to. Fortunately for all of them, the path led to a wider, more traveled path leading back to the golf course.

Holding on tightly to the ropes, Michael swayed back and forth to the movement of the vehicle as Margo accelerated and then braked in an unpredictable pattern. Margo concentrated on what was ahead of her, grasping the wheel with hands at ten and two while Chance sniffed the air and looked ahead and to the side, feeling the wind on his face. He showed no signs of being fazed by Margo's jerky, uncertain driving.

The threesome made their way up the hill and when they reached the top, they found themselves on the golf course. Margo looked both ways and crossed the fairway. With no golfers in sight, she made the decision to take the straightest and most level path home. She hoped their vehicle wouldn't leave too much of a trail. When he realized what Margo was doing, Michael was fit to be tied. If anyone saw them or discovered who tore up the course with their ATV, he would surely be barred from joining the club - or at very least be scorned by the locals. The bylaws strictly forbade crossing the course with anything but a golf cart, so they were trespassing and possibly damaging the fairways. But it was useless persuading Margo to change course once she set her plan into action. She and Chance sat in the front completely oblivious to his protestations. Michael sat back, accepting his fate or whatever came next as part of their new adventure. It would be a funny story to tell someday, he thought - but not to the locals.

Michael's back ached from sitting on the floor of the box and he had a bruised ego from Margo's superior handling of the situation. He had to admit, though, once she became accustomed to it, she drove the side-by-side smoothly across the golf course leaving only a slight dent in her wake. He hoped the trail in the soft grass would soon spring back and disappear when the greens keeper cut it. Margo drove the side-by up to the front of their house as she had seen Michael do and then she leaned over and un-snapped Chance's leash at the collar to set him free. Chance leapt out of the passenger seat and trotted around to the back to check on Michael who was sliding off the tailgate, wincing when his feet touched ground. Chance licked his hand as Michael stretched out his aching back and regained his equilibrium. His back would be fine with a little move-ment, he thought. His ego might take a little more time.

"Chance, you're spoiled rotten!" Michael patted Chance's head. Chance was sitting quietly at Michael's side. He cocked his ears forward at the mention of his name and looked up at Michael. "That's the last chance you'll get to ride in the passenger seat when I'm around!" Michael lec-tured, looking down into the dog's attentive face. Chance's head bent to one side and then the other as if he really did understand what Michael was saying. But of course he only heard, "Blah, blah. blah Chance, blah, blah, blah." So, he wagged his tail contentedly and then stood up and followed Margo to the front porch where he sat panting and smiling.

CHAPTER FOUR

Neighbour Tina Shares Her Special Cookie Recipe

Margo stood by the fence which separated their two properties, talking to Tina. It was early September and the intense heat and drought of the 'heat dome' had finally given way to the more normal temperatures. After they had been told that the evacuation order (due to the nearby wildfire) was lifted Margo and Michael came home to a parched garden with shriveled raspberries still on the canes and dried-out tomatoe vines. Nearly everything else Michael had planted with such enthusiasm had either not produced or was dried up. He did find one squash hidden under one broad leaf, which had provided shade while it developed. Michael was not one to disparage the waste of a garden season; he took his reward where he found it.

Even though the garden was devastated, the plum and pear trees seemed to have weathered the drought well. Michael put that down to a viable water table not far below the surface in the valley. There were plenty of plums and pears to pick so Margo decided she would learn to can. Her mother had canned peaches and tomatoes they bought in Okanagan by the caseload. Margo had never seen the point of it, but her mother seemed to be satisfied with her contribution to the food supply. Today, Margo was out in the backyard gathering plums into a bucket when Tina waved.

Tina and Joel, part of the wave of newly retired couples who were leaving the city to find their Shan-gri-La in the country, had bought a house one street over from Margo and Michael's place. Their backyards were separated only by a wire fence that divided the properties along the two streets. Tina was wearing a plaid jacket and old baggy jeans with natural holes and frays from wear, not from the factory. She had been working in her compost located just inside her fence line, turning it over to expose the rich layers of soil beneath the top. When Tina saw Margo picking plums, she hailed her over to where she was standing, and leaned with both hands on her long-handled spade.

"Another good day!" Tina said when Margo approached.

"It is indeed!" Margo replied. "A good day to be retired!" Tina and Margo had exchanged stories of their careers and retirement. Tina was a nurse, and Margo was a high school English teacher. This exchange had become their call and response - like when the priest says, "God be with you" and the congregations responds, "And also with you". The call and response came spontaneously to Margo and Tina who shared the glee of being recently released from their duties. They greeted each other with this call and response now, affirming their membership in an exclusive club.

Tina bent forward slightly and said, "I've baked some cookies for you. I'll give you the recipe if you like them."

"Oh?" Margo said, raising her eyebrows. That was an out-of-the-blue offer. She thought maybe Tina was just being social - the way other older women in the community had been when they arrived. Some had introduced themselves while they were walking around and saw Margo and Michael on the front swing. Others had dropped off baking and cookies with cuttings for their garden, inviting them to come to tea sometime. So Margo said, "Oh, thanks Tina, but I have enough cookies in the freezer to last all winter. Michael doesn't really have a sweet tooth and I try not to eat too many sweets. I'm watching my weight go up and up." Margo laughed.

She had a round, curvy figure and light red curly hair. Models, when she was a teen, were thin with no hips or breasts and blonde straight hair. Margo knew she would never look like that but she did try to fit in to the stereotype when she was younger. Over the years she'd embraced her body type and her light skin, which burned quickly when in the sun. She had aged well, looked younger than her years and less wrinkled than her sun-worshiping friends. Just past sixty, she looked forty-five. When she said she was retiring, many of her friends and colleagues told her she looked too young to retire. She was still in the habit of watching what she ate and stuck to a daily regimen of walking her dog, Chance.

Tina, on the other hand, was athletic looking and blonde. She was the same age as Margo but her face showed her age. She still had a youthful attitude and a mischievous twinkle in her eye. Apart from high-lighting her blond hair to distract from the grey, Tina didn't fuss much with her appearance. Like Margo, she had dispensed with the expensive manicures when she retired, striking one thing off her disposable income list. When she gardened, she wore old sweat pants and T-shirts. In a candid exchange of over-the-fence stories, Tina told Margo she has been a gardening enthusiast since she and Joel had bought their first property, an acreage outside of Peterborough.

"Oh, these are special cookies," Tina said, "You won't have any of these in your freezer," she smiled and winked.

"What do you mean - special?" Margo asked.

"They're pot cookies."

What Tina said, didn't register at first with Margo. She thought Tina meant she cooked them in a pot. "What kind of pot do you use?" She asked politely.

"It depends," Tina replied, "Whatever I can grow. This summer I grew a hybrid that gives you a nice body stone but doesn't get you too high."

"Ohhhh! Pot! You mean Marijuana!" Margo exclaimed and then covered her mouth with her hand, embarrassed at her lack of sophistication. Everyone these days, including seniors (or maybe mostly seniors) were talking about smoking pot or eating edibles. Claims about it helping ease arthritis or other aches and pains and even anxiety or depression were all over Facebook. Margo was probably the last person in the world who hadn't tried pot - not even in her youth. Michael even admitted to smoking weed when he was in high school but gave it up in university when the stakes for good grades were higher.

A twinkly giggle escape Tina's mouth. "What did you think I meant?"

"I . . . I . . . it just twigged what you meant" Margo struggled to straighten out her response. "And you're right. I don't have any in my freezer," she laughed. "But I don't think I need any just the same."

Tina leaned forward. "Are you sure you don't WANT to try them?"

"Uh . . . no. I'm fine. We don't do drugs." *That came out wrong*, Margo thought and tried to back-track, "I mean, I know its legal. And I don't care about what anyone else does, but I just don't need to have the experience, that's all."

Tina smiled. "No problem. I'm not a pusher. But in case you do want to try them sometime, I've left a bag on your deck with the recipe. I dropped it off while I was on a walk early this morning. I didn't want to disturb you and Michael so I didn't ring the bell. Just came over to tell you about it - and to say, don't eat more than one at a time - at least not until you've experienced what it's like. Wait, like, half an hour to see. They freeze just fine so if you don't want to try them now, just put them in your freezer. Who knows! You might want to try them later. They're great for insomnia and any chronic pain you might have. I use them for my back. It gets sore when I garden so I go in about four o'clock to have a cookie and a cup of tea to relax. Great stuff! But if you really don't want them, you can always bring them back. Joel or I will eat them eventually."

"I see," said Margo. She didn't see at all. Who does that? Who comes around to the neighbours and drops off pot cookies? Margo thought she had stepped into an alternate universe for a second, where seniors walked around the block with their dogs or gardened, but did you really know which ones were high. Were they all high except her and Michael? 'Michael!' she thought, 'Michael is at home. He might open the door and see the cookies and just grab one without reading the instructions. Men don't read instructions, let alone recipes!' Margo suddenly realized she had to fetch the cookies off the deck before Michael got hold of them.

"Well - thanks for thinking of us, Tina. Oh my goodness, what time is it? I have a canning pot I left boiling. I had better go and rescue it before it boils dry - and I need to get these inside." She picked up her bucket of plums and turned towards the house. Hesitating, she turned back and said, "Would you like to come and pick some plums? I noticed you don't have a plum tree, and we have so many." Margo swept her hand around the back of the garden that was littered with plums.

"Oh sure!" Tina said. "I'll do that sometime. Thanks! Enjoy your cookies!" She waved goodbye to Margo, but Margo was already striding as quickly as she dared towards the house without seeming to be in a panic - which she was.

When Margo opened the door, she called out Michael's name. He didn't answer. Setting her bucket of plums down, she ran up the stairs to the front door and opened it. The bag Tina said she left wasn't there. Now she was in a full-blown panic. Margo swept her eyes over the kitchen counters. She spied an empty plastic grocery bag on the side counter and a piece of paper beside it. She picked up the paper. It was the recipe:

½ cup pot butter (see directions for mixing pot into butter)
½ cup plain butter
1 egg
1 cup white sugar
1 cup brown sugar (packed)
1 tsp. baking powder
1 tsp. baking soda
2 cups flour
1 cup chocolate chips

When she read that far, Margo put down the recipe and looked around. Where were the cookies? And where was Michael? She called again, but heard the muted tones of music playing in Michael's music room. Michael was an audiophile. He liked to play the guitar and write songs sometimes. His songs were folksy and upbeat. Michael had said that when they moved to their retirement home, he wanted his own music room - a place he could go to and shut the door to listen to music if he liked or to play his guitar. Margo thought that was an excellent idea.

Margo ran downstairs. Michael's door was shut.

She could hear loud music playing on the stereo. She knocked and called his name. Michael appeared at the door. He still hadn't changed out of his sweats. His feet were bare and his hair was uncombed. He grinned widely when he saw Margo and leaned against the door as if he needed something to prop himself up.

"Hi Margo." he said again shaping his lips around her name as if he was talking to a deaf person who read lips.

"Hi," Margo said, curiously looking at his face. His eyes seemed to go everywhere without focusing and his head was bobbing slightly. "I called you, but you didn't answer."

Michael exaggerated a frown and looked up at the ceiling and then concentrated on looking Margo in the eyes. "You called? I guess I didn't hear you. I was down here listening to music." He said it slowly as if he had to find and grab each word out of the air and put it in his mouth. Then Michael beamed at his accomplishment of getting the words out.

He's high! Margo thought, recognizing the signs, signs she had seen countless times before in her students when they came to class stoned - usually after lunch break when they had time to go out and smoke a joint with their friends. "Are you high, Michael?" She asked.

Michael's face twisted into an exaggerated question mark. "Me? High? No! How could I be? I don't even smoke the stuff!" But next he gave himself away by laughing uncontrollably and slumping half way down the door frame.

"Are you sure you aren't?" Margo said as she put

her hand under his elbow and helped him to stand up again. She guided him over to the couch. Then she sat down herself. "Have you seen the cookies Tina set on the deck?" She asked. *He must have eaten one*, she thought.

Michael's head was resting on the back of the couch. His eyes were closed. He opened them when she asked that question. "Why yes!" he replied and tried to snap his fingers but his thumb and forefinger wouldn't coordinate. "They were delicious! Chocolate chip. You should get the recipe Margo." Then he let his head fall back.

"They were? Where are they?" Margo asked, "You didn't eat them all did you?"

"Oh, no" Michael responded without moving his head. "I just had one I think, maybe two. I brought them down with me when I came to listen to music. Man, they're good. You should get the recipe. Isn't this music great?" He closed his eyes again.

Margo looked around frantically for the cookies. Tina had said she brought over a half-dozen, just as a sample to try. Margo wanted to know how many Michael had eaten. *Could you overdose on pot*? she wondered. *What do you do for someone who O/Ds on pot cookies? Make them throw up*? That thought of having to do that turned her stomach.

She spied a plastic container on top of the stereo speaker. The lid was off. Margo slipped her hand from under Michael's back where she had been holding him upright. His body slid down sideways onto the couch and he seemed content to stay that way.

Four cookies, Margo counted. That meant

Michael had already eaten a couple. What had Tina said? Margo heard her neighbour's voice in her head, *Just try one - or even half of one - and wait until the effects kicked in before you eat any more*. Margo turned back to Michael who was slumped sideways on the couch. "Michael!" she shook his shoulders to bring him around. Michael stirred. "Michael!" she repeated. Michael struggled to right himself, blinking at her.

"Did you eat more than one of these cookies?" she asked.

Michael frowned. "I might have," he said. "But I left some for you."

Margo sighed and sat down on the couch with Michael, the plastic container in her hand. "You've eaten two pot cookies, Michael."

"I did?" Michael blinked and shook his head as if to shake off the stone.

"You did!" Margo said emphatically. "Tina told me she brought them over for us to try if we wanted. There was a recipe and instructions saying what they were. Did you read it, Michael?"

"Read what?" Michael blinked, trying to focus his eyes on his wife.

"The instructions - about what they were and how to eat them. Just half of one at a time."

"I didn't read that." Michael snorted and weaved. "Men don't read instructions." He laughed at his own joke as if it were the funniest thing he had ever heard.

Margo pursed her lips but decided that she couldn't do anything about Michael's condition. He would have to straighten up on his own. She got up to leave.

Michael sat up suddenly and grabbed Margo's arm. "Its really fun!" he said. "You should try it!" Margo pulled away. *What a ridiculous idea*, she thought. How many years had she been lecturing students about the dangers of taking drugs?

"No, I'm serious Margo!" he said. "Just try one. It won't hurt you. And you might like it. C'mon. We're retired. We don't have to go anywhere or see anyone, or be anyone. Why not! Let yourself go for once. We can listen to music together . . . come on . . . " and he patted the seat beside him on the couch.

Margo hesitated at the door. She was about to go out and close it, but she had another thought. *Why not*, she said to herself. *Michael's right. We have no place to go and no one we need to be responsible for or make a good impression upon. And we are safe in our own home and it's legal - although that shouldn't matter - no RCMP is going to knock on the door to ask us if we are doing drugs. Then she quoted Pierre Elliot Trudeau in her mind, "The government has no business in people's bedrooms."*

Margo sat down on the couch beside Michael and reached for a cookie. She chose the smallest one she could see, although there wasn't much difference, and took a bite. *Mmmm . . . not bad*! She thought. And then she took another bite and another, until she had devoured the whole thing. Then she settled down beside Michael, waiting for the effects to kick in. *I wonder how I will know when that is*? Margo thought. *Will I feel sick? Will I be able to move? Talk? Hear*?

Margo's thoughts went round and round like this, until she didn't hear them anymore. All she could hear was the music. She felt Michael beside her. Here she was a retiree, getting high for the first time in her life. A pot virgin! She giggled at the thought. Her thoughts had drifted off onto another tangent when Michael's voice startled her. She must have fallen asleep she thought. Her eyes were closed.

Michael's voice came through the fog. He said, "Isn't this a great song? I think I recognize it but I can't put my finger on where I heard it before. I wonder who the artist is. Do you know who it is Margo?"

Margo giggled. "No." She prodded him playfully. 'Get up, silly! Go find out. You know it will bug you until you do. Just walk over there, take the CD out! I can't Google it for you, babe. I don't have my phone." Did she just call her husband, 'Babe'? Margo snorted out a laugh. That was really funny, she thought. *Babe . . . I think I'm high*! And she broke into a fit of giggles.

Michael was still trying to figure out the artist they were listening to. He pushed himself off the couch and weaved slightly as he made his way to the CD player. He pressed the eject button and the music stopped. He pushed another button and the CD player whirred and spit out the CD. Michael squinted at it and held the CD up and away from his face since he didn't have his reading glasses on to help to read the label. "I can't believe this, man! It's me! I'm singing my own song! I recorded it ten years ago!" Waving the CD in his hand, Michael collapsed into the couch. They both laughed so hard their stomachs ached.

"I can't believe you didn't recognize your own tune!" Margo exclaimed.

" I didn't write it stoned!" They broke into peels of laughter again.

Later that day when they were both sitting in their matching recliners staring out the window at their backyard and their neighbours, Margo said, "I'll have to thank Tina for the cookies and the recipe when I see her next."

CHAPTER FIVE

The Teacher Gets An Education

September was a month of seasonal change in Wannatoka Springs. The days were still warm but waves of cool air wafted down the mountains, reminding the residents that summer was making a transition into fall, which came with its own beauty and duty of care to the outdoor surroundings of this mountain village. Apple, pear and plum trees, which grew in almost every yard, needed to be picked before the bears that roamed freely in this community feasted on them, breaking down fences as they barged through to get the fruit. Gardens had to be put to bed, fruit canned and bulbs planted in anticipation of spring blooms.

"A man called 'Spliff' stopped by," said Margo. It was mid-morning. Margo was peeling potatoes at the kitchen sink and putting together a crock-pot stew. Michael had just stepped in for a drink of water. He had been out in his greenhouse seeding herbs and setting up the grow lights to accommodate the shortening days of fall. He planned to grow herbs and perhaps lettuce year-round if the greenhouse maintained its heat. In late winter, early spring, he would start his tomatoes and some of the vegetables and flowers from seed.

"Spliff?" Michael repeated, raised eyebrows forming the question. He washed his hands under the tap beside Margo.

"That's how he introduced himself," she said. "He told me to pass a message on to you since you're the gardener. He has plants for sale, if you want to come take a look. Pot plants. He said he will have both kinds - one was called 'indigo' and the other that sounded like the plant-based sugar - stevia." Margo looked up. Her lips were pursed in a held-back smile and her brows knit in a frown.

Michael dried his hands on a tea towel that hung on the stove. "Oh?" he said, still perplexed. "He must've come by because I was talking to Ed on the street the other day. Ed talked about growing pot for his own use, said I should try it. He said there was a guy here that sold pot plants and would let him know I was interested if I wanted some."

"Oh Michael," Margo sighed, looking at him wiping his hands on the kitchen towel. "I've asked you time and again, please don't wash your hands in the kitchen sink when you come in from the garden." The towel was streaked with garden dirt.

Michael flipped it off the stove handle and

checked it over. "Sorry," he said and winced. "Won't happen again. I'll get you a clean towel." Michael started walking down the hall to the closet.

"So it's pot plants now, is it?" Margo queried. "You want to grow pot? You don't even do pot - well except for that one time." Margo's expression became a reproachful half-smile. Michael smiled, recalling the two of them listening to music and giggling like a couple of teenagers all afternoon.

He shrugged. "I thought I'd see how it goes," Michael said. "Just a gardener's curiosity. I don't plan on smoking the stuff or becoming a pot-head or anything."

"Sure you won't," Margo whispered to herself, since Michael had walked out of hearing distance - which wasn't too far these days, she noticed. He said she spoke too softly but she was sure he was losing his hearing. Either way, she found she had to either accentuate her words and say them to his face when he said, "Pardon? I didn't hear you."

When Margo finished putting the stew together and setting the crock-pot so the stew would be ready in time for supper, she thought she would go outside to read on the deck. The September sun slanted beneath the overhanging roof in the afternoon, making it a perfect time to lounge on the porch swing while sipping a cup of tea and reading a book.

She was in a supine position, shielding her eyes with her elbow, reading from her e-reader when she heard a loud ATV. There were a surprising number of ATVs that traveled up and down the quiet streets of their community. Neighbours traveled ponderously down the street to visit with other neighbours, waving at whoever was out on their porches as they passed. When Margo went on a walk with her dog, Chance, she came upon groups of them at a neighbour's house straddling their ATV or sitting in the driver's seat of their side-by-side, drinking coffee or beer (whichever they were inclined to bring with them) and chatting with the neighbour on whose lawn they were parked.

      The ATVers were almost always men. Margo wondered about that. You would think in the 21st century, the birth of the 'Me Too' women's movement, more women would put their peddle to metal and say, "Me too! I want to ride around in a slow-moving vehicle and stop to chat and drink a beer with my neighbours." But it seemed that most women in Wannatoka Springs walked. Sometimes they walked with their dog, and sometimes with another woman and their dogs. When they got to a familiar neighbour's house and found them sitting on their porch or working in the front garden, they would stop and have a chat. They would release their dogs, if their dog and the neighbour's dog were friends. The dogs would romp and play - a 'play date' they called it and they beamed at the two dogs like they were their children, chasing each other around the yard while the women amicably chatted for a while before the walker would make her excuses and say a pleasant good bye.

      So, women walked. Men rode ATVs. And Margo thought this was a good indicator of which sex would outlive the other.

Margo stretched and turned her head towards the sound of the ATV that was making it's way slowly and noisily up the street. Riding the side-by-side was an older heavy-set man - although who could judge who was older in this community of pensioners. To Margo he looked to be anywhere from sixty-five or eighty. He had thin, salt and pepper hair sticking out of his camouflage cap on both sides and was caught up by a black elastic band into a wispy three-inch ponytail, if you could call it that. His face was weathered and flaccid. Spidery red veins on his cheeks and nose gave away the signs of a heavy drinker, Margo thought. Curiously alert, his bright blue eyes darted everywhere, taking in everything. He wore work a camo jacket - a different print than the hat, work jeans and a faded T-shirt that looked like it used to be black. His work boots were as faded as his T-shirt. Riding along with him, in the passenger seat, was a six foot marijuana plant in a large pot pinned to the floor with a brick.

The vehicle came to a stop on the street in front of Margo. The man didn't dismount. Instead he left his ATV running and shouted out his side of the conversation from the driver's seat. "Hello!" He called out in a rolling voice, one hand waving and the other gripping the steering wheel as he leaned out.

Margo sat up and edged to the front of the swing and planted her feet. The swing stopped rocking. "Hi!" she answered, shading her eyes. "It's Spliff, isn't it?"

The man's smile broadened. "Spliff, here," he

answered. He likely hadn't heard Margo's greeting so he was ad-libbing what someone would say when he pulled up. "Michael wouldn't happen to be home would he?"

"Oh, sorry, you just missed him," Margo said in a loud voice as she rose from her sitting position to walk closer to the man who cocked his head sideways towards her. He, like almost everyone she had met seemed to be slightly deaf. Margo approached the ATV. "Looks like you got a Marijuana plant there," she said, eying up the tall, ferny plant.

"Yup," Spliff said. "She's a beauty. Know anything about marijuana plants, Margo?" He didn't wait for an answer. "This here's a Diesel Haze. Female. She's a Sativa strain." Stroking the plant's fronds with one hand, he looked at it with affection. Once he started he couldn't be stopped. Spliff went on with a road-side lecture on types and strains of marijuana plants, their sexes, what they were grown for - recreational or medicinal purposes, how they liked to be treated and so on. Margo was stunned at the breadth and depth of Spliff's knowledge. *Don't judge a book by its cover,* she thought. *Or by its age.* Spliff completed his roadside lecture with an inquiry, "What kind of imbiber are you and Michael?" Margo was stumped.

"I don't - I mean we don't - imbibe at all, or not much really," she said, limply shrugging her shoulders. She didn't know how to respond to this man's obvious passion for growing marijuana plants. On the one hand he seemed affable and she wanted to be friendly with him as he was a neighbour and this was a small village. On the other, he seemed like a door-to-door pot salesman at the very least. She didn't want to get trapped into buying something she wouldn't use. In the next sentence, he quelled at least one of her concerns.

"I don't sell the final product." Spliff said, confidentially leaning over toward Margo, tipping his weight out of the side-by and hanging on to the roll bar so gravity wouldn't pull him down. He straightened up and said, "I just sell the plants. I like to grow 'em, experiment with different types, cross-pollinate. That's my interest. I don't imbibe much myself, but I supply plants to local gardeners here. You'll find that most of your neighbours except for - here he paused and leaned forward and said in a conspiratorial tone - your Christian neighbours next door who still think it's a sin. He cocked his head towards their house. "No one told them yet that there is pot in Heaven. They don't know that's why they call it Heaven." And he snorted a laugh at his own joke. Margo smiled in return but had no idea what was funny about it. She crossed her arms in front of her. She was nervous but didn't want to appear naive.

"So how much do you want for a plant?" she asked, hoping to make a quick deal that would satisfy Spliff and get him to move on. She wouldn't feel guilty at all disposing of it later if it didn't cost too much.

"They start at twenty dollars. He reached into the back of the side-by, grunting with the effort and pulled out a four inch plant in a plastic seedling cup. "This cute little girl is all you need for casual recreation for you and Michael." He winked. Margo winced and stepped back. She was unused to the pungent odour of pot. "Oh she'll grow tall if you let her, but she should be trimmed so she doesn't get too leggy to produce."

Margo knew she was in too deep. She knew nothing of how to sex a pot plant or how to grow it or what was important about it, but she didn't want to offend Spliff either so she said, offhandedly, "Twenty dollars? OK. I think I can afford that - as long as it doesn't get to be a weekly habit!" she laughed nervously at her own joke.

Spliff smiled and said, "Sure, but you'll want this little one too." And he reached around and pulled another plant from a different tray. "She's called Moon-Dance. A hy-bird."

Margo couldn't see the difference between the two plants but she was sure Spliff would explain. One word stuck in her English teacher head, "Hy-bird?" she asked out loud.

"Yeah - hy-bird. That's the kind that you cross so it can have babies all on its own but can't reproduce itself.

"Oh!" said Margo, "hybrid."

"That's right," Spliff said, "hy-bird. Ya learn somethin' new every day don't ya? Good to keep learnin'. Its' what keeps you young in the mind." He tapped his head and grinned.

Margo smiled back. She remembered that she

had retired from being an English teacher so it was no longer her job to correct people's English grammar or spelling.

"I'll take both," she said. "Just hang on right there, uh - Spliff. I'll just nip inside and get you some cash. "Forty dollars?"

"For you," Spliff said, "and because you and Michael are new to this neighbourhood, I'll give you a first-time price of thirty dollars for two."

Sure, thought Margo as she retraced her steps to the deck and went inside to grab some cash from her purse, *now he really does sound like a pusher. First time deal gets them hooked and then full price and by the way, due to supply and demand - the price just went up*. She didn't want to admit it, but there was a spring in her step and she felt a sense of adventure going into the up-till-recently shady, illegal enterprise in Canada. And here she was a retired schoolteacher.

Margo handed Spliff the cash and he handed her the plants. "Now you tell Michael, these here clones do real well in a greenhouse. If he wants, he can plant them in spring when he sets out his tomatoes. That would be about the right time." With that, he put his ATV in gear, and as he rolled out he put his finger at the side of his nose and tapped it. "I'll be around if Michael needs some advice."

As Spliff rolled off, Margo held the plants in her hands looking after him and, for some reason, thought of Santa Claus delivering presents to good girls and boys. She shook her head and smiled to herself as she walked back to the deck and set them down carefully as she would babies - which they were.

Michael came in from the greenhouse, washed his hands dutifully in the laundry room sink and walked into the kitchen to have a cup of coffee with Margo, a routine they started in their retirement. He was standing beside the coffeemaker waiting for it to heat up and gazing out at his front lawn, deciding whether to cut it again or not - when he noticed the two little pot plants on the deck.

"What the hell?" he exclaimed, and startled when Margo came up from behind.

"I got an education today on how to grow Marijuana plants," Margo said. "Spliff came around while I was reading on the deck. So I bought a couple. I thought you should try growing them since it seems to be the thing to do here." She shrugged nonchalantly as if this was as usual as saying she bought tulip bulbs.

Michael stared out at the plants for a second or two.

"Meet Diesel and Moon-Dance." Margo said, putting her arm around Michael's waist. "They are companion plants."

"Is that so," Michael said.

"It is. And . . . I learned a new word today," Margo said, laughing. "Hy-bird. Did you know that hy-bird is a type of marijuana plant that has sex with itself so it can produce buds but can't reproduce? Spliff pronounces it 'hy-bird'. Isn't that cute?"

"Yeah, cute," Michael said, his mind still reeling. "So this is what this straight-arrow retired couple from the city is becoming? Pot growers in the Kootenays?" Michael shrugged and sighed in resignation. "I'll plant them in my garden and see what happens." Then he settled into his recliner to read.

"Coffee?" Margo came up behind Michael with two cups of freshly expressed coffees and steamed milk. The two of them walked out to the front porch and settled down on the swing, sitting with their new companions.

CHAPTER SIX

And Roscoe Makes Four

"Yeow!" Michael heard as he slumped down on the couch. He liked to read using a throw cushion to prop up his head. Startled at the sound coming from what he thought was the pillow, Michael arched his back and sat straight up, looking behind him to see what had protested.

A large grey cat uncurled himself in the crook of the couch's arm and stared at Michael, ears back eyes accusing the intruder of disturbing his nap. When he glanced at the couch before he lay down, Michael's brain had registered that there was something different about that pillow. For one thing it was plush. Margo liked to change out the decorative pillows on the couch, along with other accessories. Every few months, she would 'spruce up the decor', as she put it. It was cheaper by far than buying new furniture and caused less chaos than painting the walls. She donated the ones she replaced to the charity shops since neither

Margo nor Michael liked clutter.

"Margo?" Michael called out as he got up of the couch, looking down at the cat. The cat curled back into its snoozing configuration, head tucked in paws, one eye open to see what Michael's next move would be.

"Margo?" Michael called again, walking downstairs. "Are you home?"

"Down here!" came Margo's voice. "I'm doing a load of wash!"

Michael skipped down the stairs and found Margo sitting in a chair in the TV room, reading a book.

"How was your golf game today?" She asked, smiling benignly. "Did you best your last score?"

"Uh . . . good." Michael answered. He ran his hand through his hair and asked, "Do we have a cat, Margo? I just found one on the couch, sitting in my spot."

"Oh!" Margo said, "Yes. We now have a cat. His name is Roscoe. I'm sorry Michael. I didn't hear you come in or I would have met you upstairs and introduced you."

"What?" Michael was astonished that Margo would make a snap decision about a four-legged addition to the family. Before they adopted Chance as a puppy, they discussed at length, what breed of dog they wanted and what size it should be.

Retirement was bringing out a new side of Margo. She was going off on her own more, exploring local places like the farm in their community with the sign that had eggs for sale. She came home with a dozen farm fresh eggs and talked enthusiastically about raising chickens.

Michael pointed out that they knew nothing about chickens and the eggs were reasonably priced, conveniently just down the road, so it made sense just to buy the eggs and let the farmers do the work.

Earlier that day, Margo had driven into Crystal Lake to buy groceries and stop in at the farmer's market to pick up some fresh vegetables. It was always a social time. She liked to stop to talk to the vendors and crafters about their work, gleaning tips and learning more about the lifestyle and mindsets of the people of the Kootenays.

Margo had brought home a number of surprisingly random things lately claiming they would be part of some sort of project she would work on when the weather became cooler, but why a cat? Michael wondered. And why this cat? It was obviously a full-grown, rather well fed, sedentary animal that had an already established attitude. Besides that, he was a longhair. Michael visualized the future: constantly vacuuming the couch and other fabric upholstery and drapes to get rid of the cat hair. And stretching the vacuum hose to get into the corners where the fur gathered in floating islands that attracted even more hair.

"So what's the story about the cat?" Michael asked Margo, crossing his arms at his chest. He was holding back his judgment but was annoyed.

Margo stood up and walked over to Michael with open arms and put both hands on Michael's shoulders. "Oh, don't be mad, Michael. It was a spontaneous decision. There wasn't time to consult you. And Roscoe is going to be a perfect companion for me in retirement." She rolled the 'r' in perfect so it sounded like 'purrfect'.

Michael was a still as a statue. "What do you mean, you didn't have time to consult me?"

"Well, it's a long story. I'll tell you about it." Margo started to talk fast, something she did when she knew she needed to keep the reasoning short to get it in before Michael could object. "But first I want to say that Roscoe will be my responsibility." Margo started. "I will change the litter box, feed him, brush him and vacuum up the hair. You won't have to do a thing for him. And you can see that he doesn't need a lot of attention. I don't have to take him for walks. He sleeps most of the day." Margo went on detailing how she would take care of her new foundling, assuring Michael that Rosco would be no trouble and all Margo's responsibility. "I'll make a little bed for him with cushions on the floor and take him down here when I'm working on projects. I'm sure he'll love sleeping next to the wood stove in the winter."

"That's all well and good, Margo. But a cat? You never said you wanted a cat. What's the story?"

Margo giggled nervously. "Why don't we sit down here and I'll tell you the story." She patted the couch in the TV room. Michael took a seat, and stiffly crossed one leg over the other, hands clasped around his knee.

"OK. I'm listening."

Margo sat down beside Michael and took a deep breath before launching into her story about how she came to take Roscoe home with her that day.

She had found him at the indoor Saturday market at the fire hall in Crystal Lake, she explained. He was in a cat carrier at the foot of one of the tables where an elderly woman's home knit crafts were displayed. She had gone to the fire hall for lunch and to pick up some fresh vegetables.

The volunteer women there made the best homemade soup to help raise funds for the fire hall. She was walking around with her soup in a take-away bowl and was admiring the knitted dishrags and pot-holders when she heard a distressed "meow" at her feet. She looked down and saw the eyes and ears of a large, grey cat in the carrier. The hand-written sign taped to the table above the carrier read. "Roscoe. Male cat. Fixed. Currently homeless. Approx. eight-years-old. His owner passed away. Free to take away."

Margo looked up at the elderly lady who was knitting complacently behind the table. "Do you know anything about this cat?" she inquired.

"No, not really," the woman said, "Just that his name is Roscoe and he was found in the home of one of the ladies who used to be a volunteer here. Mable Whiting was her name. Such a dear soul. She will be missed. She silk-screened scarves. Maybe you've seen them here?"

Margo nodded her head. She remembered the beautiful scarves and had thought of coming back to buy one someday.

"Anyway, Mable lived alone with her cat. When she didn't show up for the craft sale last Saturday someone went round to see if she was OK and found her on the couch with the TV still on. Must've been there for a few days, they said. Awful business. Anyway, this here cat, Roscoe, she pointed with her head, keeping her eyes on her knitting the whole time, "Wouldn't you know he was curled up beside her! Didn't want to leave his mistress even at the end." She sighed and shook her head, stopping her two-handed rhythm to wipe away a tear and then went on. "She didn't have any relations," she said. "And none of us want to take on a cat. Too old myself. What if that happened to me? Roscoe, poor dear, might be traumatized. PTSD even. Do you believe cats can have PTSD?" She looked up at Margo, hands still moving automatically. Her needles clicking at an even pace.

Margo didn't know, so she just shook her head and said, "Poor thing. That's tragic."

"Indeed it is." The elderly woman shrugged her shoulders. "So now he has no place to go. There's no animal shelter around here so we are hoping some-one with a big heart will take him. There's plenty of life in him yet, and he is a calm cat unless something's got him riled up - and then you have to watch out, apparently."

The story went straight to Margo's heart. She bent down to look at the cat. It blinked back at her in-differently, let out a muffled "meow" and rolled onto his side. Margo noticed that he was almost too big for the cage.

Margo stood up and said matter-of-factly, "I can give Roscoe a good home. How about I finish my rounds and come back for him."

The elderly woman smiled, showing the few teeth she had left and said, "If you want him, you are certainly welcome to take him with you. No charge. Bless you."

Margo finished her soup, trashed the container and came back to the woman's booth. She felt guilty that she was getting a cat for free so she picked up a knitted dishcloth and asked, "How much do you want for this?"

"Eight dollars," the lady said, "Hand knit by myself. Very popular. You'll never use anything else to wash up with once you tried it."

"I'll take one." Eight dollars for a bit of yarn and what looked like fifteen minutes of work seemed high to Margo but she reasoned that the woman probably supplemented her pension with it, so Margo handed her a twenty. "Keep the change and thanks for taking care of Roscoe! I'll take it from here."

Michael was incredulous when he heard the story. "So you just went shopping at the farmer's market and picked up an old cat? Like you would pick up a dozen eggs or a bunch of lettuce?"

Margo's bravado began to crack. She knew this impulsive behaviour was unlike her and she didn't know how to defend the decision in a rational way. It wasn't a rational decision. Under Michael's quizzical stare, Margo covered her face with her hands. She was embarrassed and regretful.

"It was an impulse. That isn't like me, I know. But nothing about this experience of retirement is like me." She removed her hands from her face, took a deep breath, and wiped tears that were starting to trickle from her eyes. "The truth is, Michael, ever since we retired and moved here, I have been yearning for something to take care of, to put my energy into, like I did for my students. You've adapted well to life in retirement. You play golf. You have your garden. I don't know why, but none of those things strike me as ways I can find fulfillment in this new life. So, voila! I found a cat! I read somewhere that petting a cat, listening to and feeling its purr is a calming therapy. They are good companions. Anyway, when I saw this poor cat, cramped up in his carrier, I felt so much compassion for him. And I just wanted to cuddle him and pet him and listen to him purr."

"But we have Chance. You can pet him anytime. He is always looking for your attention." He was tempted to give Margo an ultimatum about taking the cat back to wherever it came from or re-homing it - but the words caught in his throat when he saw the sadness and hopefulness in his wife's eyes.

"I know, but a dog isn't a cat," Margo said faintly, and looked away.

The appeal in her voice and her emotional demonstration were new to Michael and new for Margo, too. The pre-retirement Margo would have held his gaze with fierce eyes that dared him to cross her. But then, the Margo he had lived with for most of his adult life would have been pre-occupied with school. Coming home every night chatting about what a student accomplished, or complaining about what a kid had done to disrupt her day and how she had to work through it - sometimes with parents and the principal. Her work was done in community. She had department committee meetings to organized, books to read and lessons to plan. Her evenings were almost as full of work she brought home. She was a scheduler and a planner. Her reward was the difference she was making in her students' learning.

Now, Margo had the freedom from responsibility and planning her time. She could do anything she liked. But she had stepped away from what she loved. Instead she collected random items she thought she might use in projects. And she often lost interest in them before she started or shortly afterwards. She was becoming less rigidly organized and more spontaneous. She was trying things she would have dismissed before. She was trying to find meaning for herself in this post-retirement phase of her life. Finding meaning in retirement didn't come in a ready-made package. The self-help books Margo had studied in preparation for this period of her life had given her superficial goals and explanations for what she could anticipate, but none could have prepared her for the unique experience she felt but could not easily express. At this moment in time, she had gravitated to something that needed taking care of, who relied on her and kept her company while she figured out what she wanted from this stage of her life.

Michael uncrossed his legs and stood up, facing Margo, hands outstretched inviting her to take them. She put her hands in his and he gently pulled her up from her seat. Wrapping his arms around her and holding her close, he said, "Why don't you come upstairs and properly introduce me to Roscoe. We had an informal introduction when I tried to use him for a pillow under my head. But he didn't take too kindly to that." He smiled.

Margo moved away to study said Michael's face for marks. "He didn't scratch you did he? I also didn't tell you he has a bad temper when he is disturbed."

"Uh - no," Michael said. "He just scowled at me and warned me to get off him or else! So I did - quickly!"

Margo laughed in spite of herself. "I was warned that Roscoe came with a bit of an attitude. But mostly he just sleeps and likes to cuddle on the couch or on the bed."

"No," Michael said, "I draw the line at the cat sleeping with us on the bed. The couch - OK. but not the bed."

"Of course," said Margo, nodding seriously. "Don't worry. I'll read Roscoe the riot act. No sleeping on the bed." Then Margo looked at Michael and said, "Thanks. Michael," and kissed him on the lips.

"For what?" Michael's face lightened. He took Margo's affection as a sign that she was pulling herself out of her doldrums. The old Margo was surfacing again.

"I really thought you were going to make a fuss."

"I thought of doing that, actually," Michael said, cocking his head to one side and lifting one brow. "But you let me play with the ATV and eat funny cookies, so what can I say? We both have to discover what makes us tick in this new adventure."

Michael held Margo out at arm's length and

added, "But can we draw the line at large stock animals and chickens please?"

Margo laughed. "Oh! You didn't see the goat in the backyard?"

Michael started. He glanced toward the window for one second and stopped.

"Gottcha!" Margo said merrily. "And, yes, we can draw the line at stock animals and chickens. Come and meet Roscoe," she said, and took Michael's hand to lead him upstairs where Roscoe had resumed his favorite position.

Margo loved having a cat. And Roscoe loved Margo's company. The two of them became inseparable. If she was downstairs, he was perched somewhere close by sleeping on the chair or material she had sorted into piles on the craft table. If she was upstairs, he was curled up beside her, or on her lap if she was in her reclining chair reading. Margo was faithful with what she said she would do and took care of all of Roscoe's needs. Michael adapted to having a cat in the house, even though he was annoyed every time he had to brush off the cat hair from his pants.

Roscoe became part of the decor more than anything. He did sleep most of the time, usually on the couch. He never did take to the bed Margo made up for him downstairs. But then, cats don't like to be told what to do, even if it's what they would have done if you hadn't suggested it. Most nights he could be found curled up beside Margo on the bed. He knew enough to wait until Michael was asleep to tuck up close with Margo, who liked to reach out and pet him in the night, and feel his purr against her stomach.

Occasionally Michael would feel him beside Margo and try to push him off but Roscoe would emit a low, threatening growl and make himself deadweight. If Michael did manage to move him off the bed, Roscoe would wait till Michael fell back to sleep and return to his place next to Margo. If Michael tried to shut him out by closing the bedroom door at night, Roscoe would make a fuss. He meowed in protest and scratched underneath the door as if trying to open it. Eventually Michael acquiesced.

Their dog Chance never had a chance with Roscoe. Upon their initial introduction when Chance romped up to Roscoe thinking that here was a new plaything he could chase around just for fun; Roscoe set him straight. Like two boxers eying each other up, Chance started out by prancing around Roscoe who was sitting on the couch glaring at him. Roscoe emitted a warning growl. Chance mistook that as a sign he wanted to play so he stuck his nose close to Roscoe and tried to sniff him. Roscoe surprised him with a left hook into his nose. Chance yipped in surprise and then ran circles around the couch, pawing his nose.

After that, Chance and Roscoe were on polite terms. If Roscoe was sleeping on Chance's bed when he went there for a nap, Chance would stretch out on the floor beside his bed, so as not to intrude on Roscoe's nap. If Roscoe wanted to go outside, Chance would be right behind him, sniffing his butt until Roscoe would turn around and glare at him. Then he'd back off to a polite distance and wait for the cat to sniff at the open door, making up his mind if he wanted to go outside or not. When Roscoe made up his mind that he would, Chance followed him out.

Soon everyone made room for the addition to the family and life settled into a casual routine. Margo worked on a couple of projects in her sewing room while Roscoe curled up beside her in the chair. Michael continued to enjoy working in his garden, going for rides on his ATV, and napping on the couch in the afternoon - with Roscoe at his head, curled up on the arm of the sofa.

CHAPTER SEVEN

The Fattest Cat in the Practice

In no time at all Roscoe had settled in. For the most part he had become a moving, but not easily movable, soft furniture accessory. He could be found curled up sleeping on the couch or on the bed like a throw cushion, or sitting on the window ledge. Occasionally his ears twitched and his head swiveled as he followed a bird's flight path across the window. He also liked to sit on Margo's craft table, but only when she was working there. The places he found most comfortable were her fabric pile and the space on her desk behind her laptop when she was using it to write the memoir she had always wanted to write. Margo didn't mind because he kept her company. He contributed the comfort of a living, breathing body that stared at what she was doing with little curiosity and no opinion.

Other than choosing his next place to lounge or take a cat nap, his movements were limited to taking care of the basic necessities - grazing at the kibble in his food bowl and using the litter box.

Michael had become used to sharing his corner of the couch with Roscoe in the morning when he drank his coffee and read the news on his phone. Since the first day of Roscoe's introduction into their home, when Michael had nearly sat on him, the ritual of sharing the corner of the couch that both had claimed as their own, became a kind of bond between them although neither admitted they liked each other's company. Invariably when Michael sat down in that corner, Roscoe would be there curled up against the padded arm. Michael would snug up close to Roscoe and deliberately reach over him with exaggerated effort to set his coffee on the side table. Then he would settle in to read, his elbow resting on the arm of the couch pinning Roscoe. Roscoe's only escape from the pressure would be to jump off the couch, which was what Michael wanted him to do. But Roscoe refused to move. Michael didn't give way either. He wasn't going to let a cat dictate where he could sit by claiming the space first. And so they sat there together, body pressed against body, pretending to ignore each other. Occasionally Roscoe would stretch out his paws, pressing against Michael's side with all four of his legs. But neither of them gave an inch.

One morning Michael was sitting on the couch having his habitual read and coffee with Roscoe and Margo was standing at the espresso machine waiting for her first cup of coffee, when suddenly the air was punctuated with an uncharacteristic exclamation that shattered the convivial silence of their morning ritual.

"Boy your ass is getting fat!"

Hearing Michael's exclamatory statement startled Margo at first, but as the accusation hit her full force she whirled around. "You talking to me, Michael?"

Margo had turned so fast that she took the cup she was holding under the espresso stream with her and coffee splashed onto her fingers. Margo let out a yelp and put down the coffee mug to suck on her burning fingers.

Michael was startled himself. Hearing Margo's accusative question followed by a scream of pain, he spun around on the couch to face her. In doing so, his knee squashed Roscoe's soft body. Enraged, Roscoe responded by digging his claws into Michael's leg.

Michael's face turned ashen, "No! No! No!" he replied emphatically, while trying to extract the claws that had penetrated the fabric of his sweat pants and were digging into his thigh. He winced and jerked Roscoe's claws out of the fabric and pushed him towards the floor. Roscoe landed with an unceremonious thud. Giving Michael the evil eye from where he landed, Roscoe arched his back and hissed a warning, then began grooming himself as if nothing notable had happened.

"No, not you at all!" Michael knew when Margo was mad. And this was one of those times. "I was talking to the cat! Sorry, my love, you are not getting fat. Your ass is perfect. Just as it always has been. Michael immediately stood up and, walking towards his wife, stretching out his arms in a pleading gesture.

Turning to the sink, Margo ran cold water on her scalded fingers. "I'm letting myself go aren't I," she said, and strained her neck to looked behind her, trying to visualize what she looked like from behind.

"No," Michael said, reaching his arms around his wife's back and giving her a tender hug. Out of the corner of his eye, he spied Roscoe sauntering over to his bowl, rooting around in his kibble, picking out the nuggets he prized, grinding them one at a time between his teeth.

Michael stared at Roscoe. "Don't you think Roscoe is getting fat? I think he is even bigger than he was when you brought him home. And he was a big boy then."

Margo looked at Roscoe who was contentedly munching through a full bowl of kibble. It had become Margo's habit to keep the bowl full so she didn't have to listen to him complain when it was empty. It was easier that way, but she had to admit, when his head disappeared into the bowl like that, ass end up, he did look like he should be preceded with a wide-load sign.

"I don't know what else to do," Margo said. "I feed him or he sets up a verbal protest until I do."

"Why don't you take him to the vet," Michael offered. "He probably could use a check-up anyway just to see if everything is OK. He might not be vaccinated or dewormed. At very least the vet could tell you how his health is and maybe give you some tips about his diet."

Margo agreed. She had thought of taking Roscoe to the vet since she brought him home, just to get a base-line health report and maybe vaccinations, although since Roscoe had no interest in going outside, she didn't think they were necessary.

Margo made the appointment with the only vet in the area, who had a rural practice up the highway from Crystal Lake. She added the date and time of the appoint-ment and the link to the location she found on Maps into her phone calendar and set the reminder for the day before. Since she was retired, she found that often one day blurred into the next so she thought she would need a whole day's advance notice to mentally register the day and prepare for the appointment.

On the day of their appointment Margo packed Roscoe into the carrier and Michael carried him in his carrier to the car.

"This guy is heavy!" Michael said, straining to stay upright and balanced with the effort. Roscoe didn't help. His weight shifted from one side to the other as the carrier swayed with Michael's gait. Inside, Roscoe expressed his fury and the indignity of being handled this way - in a series of yowls and growls and hisses.

Margo held the door open and Michael slid the carrier with the disgruntled Roscoe into the back seat of the car.

"Sure you don't need me to come along to haul this beast to the vet's office?"

"We'll be fine," Margo said. "I can mange Roscoe myself. But I do like to see you doing it. It makes you look all manly!" And she gave Michael a light pat on his butt.

She had become more playful, Michael noticed, since she had retired. It was as if she had peeled off that outer layer of armour that had restricted her before. Michael liked to see the new Margo emerging - even if it did throw him off guard sometimes.

"OK," he said as held the driver's side door open for her, "Don't bring anymore homeless pets home with you, though!"

Margo smiled and promised she wouldn't. Then Margo and Roscoe set off on the road that took them from Wannatoka Springs to Crystal Lake, 60 kilometers away. The route wound along the shore of the lake. The sun had come out from behind the clouds and was bouncing playfully off the lake on one side of the road and on the mountain side. The forests changed from brilliantly lit to deep shadows as the road wound through them. Margo had to pinch herself to be sure it wasn't just a dream. Wannatoka Springs was home.

As she drove through the main street of Crystal Lake, Margo noted the now familiar shops and restaurants. The unpretentious Kootenay Co-op grocery store re-purposed from an old barn that traded in fresh, organic vegetables, locally sourced meat, and various naturally derived treatments for whatever ailed you.

Down the street was Hurley's restaurant where Margo and Michael ate lunch when they went to Crystal Lake on their weekly shopping trip. Hurley's had the best burgers and fries according to an informal poll Margo took among her neighbours.

The only chain supermarket provided most of the staples and had become their target for weekly grocery shopping. There was an assortment of businesses and specialty shops on the main street, pet supplies, a bicycle shop, artisan wares and international clothing from exotic places like Indonesia and Thailand and a Bon Marche - dollar store. All were locally owned, no franchises. The town had maintained its small town feel through the years by not inviting fast food chains and big box stores to clutter up their streets and compete with the local businesses.

The vet was 5 kilometers past the town along the highway that ran through it. Margo saw the plain wooden sign on her left, 'Crystal Lake Veterinary Clinic', and turned onto an unpaved road that wound up a very long drive. The clinic was a nondescript, rectangular building with white walls, but the pastoral backdrop was spectacular. Behind it was a flat green and yellow field where she could see a couple of horses and a few cows grazing. Beyond the field rose a gentle range of snow-capped mountains. With the sun shining, it looked like a mountain farm in some faraway place like the Swiss Alps. Two cars were parked, facing the wooden railing that led down the path to the vet clinic. Margo parked beside the outside one. A sign just past the first car indicated that all pets must be leashed or contained.

When she opened the back passenger door and looked into his cage, Margo met Roscoe's eyes glaring at her through the bars of the carrier door. She struggled to slide Roscoe's carrier forward. He protested the movement as loudly he had the drive, with deep yowls and growls.

Grabbing the handle on top of the crate with both hands, she heaved it out of the car and hip-checked the door closed. The shifting cargo inside was getting heavier with every step. Keeping her eye on the entrance door Margo slowly made progress towards it. Roscoe didn't help - shifting his weight from side to side.

At the entrance, above the doorbell there was a sign that read, 'Ring for service'. Margo set the carrier down with a thud and straightened her back to push the buzzer. The receptionist, a plump woman with a round cherub-like face answered the door. Margo guessed she was in her forties, married with a couple of kids. She looked at Margo with raised eyebrows and smiled kindly, "Do you have an appointment?"

"Yes, we are booked in to see Dr. Staples at 1 p.m. I'm Margo and this is my cat, Roscoe."

The woman's face registered her recognition of the name and her smile widened. "Roscoe! Yes, we've been waiting for you!" She stooped down to peer at Roscoe who hissed at her when he saw her face through the grid.

"You're a big boy!" she said to Roscoe. "Let's get a weight on you." She hefted the carrier up to her hip and balanced it if it were a resistant child she was carrying in from the playground. As she carried her cargo, she said over her shoulder to Margo, "My name is Vanessa. I'm Dr. Staple's assistant, receptionist, basically all around support staff. Just close the door behind you, will you please? You can take a seat over there." Vanessa nodded her head to one side indicating a row of orange molded plastic chairs. At the weigh scale in the reception area of the office, she swung the carrier down and set it gently on the floor.

Vanessa squatted down beside the carrier and faced Roscoe through the wire window, her hand on the door latch. Still talking to him in a soothing voice, she said. "Ohhh . . . . you are one pissed off big boy aren't you, Roscoe. That's OK big fella. I'm not going to hurt you. You can relax those claws now and smooth down that fur."

Vanessa opened the cage door slowly and kept talking in that soothing, motherly voice that she must have used on her children, Margo thought, to lull them into complacency. "No need to growl at me Roscoe. I got you." Vanessa extended one hand into Roscoe's carrier, letting it hang in front of him so he could sniff it. "There now, see? You and me are going to be friends, not enemies. You're not going to bite and scratch my arm and I'm not going to put you in gunnysack and dump you in the lake. We're just going to play nice, aren't we?" Margo was startled by Vanessa's chatter, but she could see that her tone was mesmerizing to Roscoe. He didn't even struggle when she pulled him out by the scruff of his neck. "There, there, you're not going to fight me are you? And I'm not going to put a plastic bag over your head and suffocate you."

Margo was shocked at the suggestions Vanessa was making. "Excuse me," she interjected, "Do you have to talk to my cat that way?"

"Oh, yes," the woman said, smiling and still speaking in the same soothing tone. "Cats are suspicious creatures. They think that when you take them to the vet, you are there to drop them off to be exterminated. I like to reassure them that won't be the case and that we will take care of them."

"What possible difference can it make what you say?" Margo asked, "Cat's don't understand a word we say - unless it's something like 'Dinner'!"

"We don't know that," the receptionist said, as she gently placed Roscoe on the platform of the scale and scratched him behind his ear. "They may ignore what we say, and they may not do what we ask, but they do eavesdrop. Why else do you think they make such a fuss when we start talking about going to the vet with them, and scream and holler in protest all the way there?"

Margo had to think about that. She wondered if the cat overheard Michael saying he had a fat ass, and if that had given him a complex or just made him mad.

"Oh!" Vanessa exclaimed when she eyed up Roscoe's number on the scale. "What a big boy! You're

9.97 kilograms. You are the weight of a lynx, your wildcat brother. Did you know that? Except you are not your brother lynx. You don't climb trees or hunt. You don't have to even lift a paw to get your food do you. Your person brings it right to you, especially when you beg. You have your person trained, don't you. She'll give in to your demands or you create a fuss. And you sit on the couch all day. So, you're this big because you are spoiled and entitled and lazy." She kept up this one-sided conversation with Roscoe in a sweet, soothing voice as she slipped him back into his carrier without a single protest.

Now she's aiming her comments at me, Margo thought. *She knows I can understand her very well.* Margo was about to protest her indignation when they were interrupted.

An inside door opened and a man appeared abruptly. He was blinking at Margo as if he had just stepped into daylight after spending some time in the dark. Margo stood up to greet him and extended her hand. "You must be . . . "

" . . . Dr. Staples, the veterinarian." The man finished her sentence and, without taking her hand to shake, turned to Vanessa who was back at her desk, updating the file she had started for Roscoe. He appeared to be in his mid-fifties. He was short for a man and had a small frame. His thinning greyish brown hair was combed over from one side to the other, the strands neatly stuck together with some kind of hairdressing. He looked over his gold-rimmed aviator glasses when he glanced at Margo and then down at Roscoe. Then he pushed them up his nose with one finger. After a brief inspection of the cat in the carrier, he picked up a blue file folder on the corner of Vanessa's desk. Opening it, he read the name, "Roscoe? Is that you?" He looked at Margo.

"Uh no, I'm Margo," Margo said. "This is Roscoe." She stood by the carrier and opened her hand to demonstrate, "My cat."

"I can see it's a cat. Does Roscoe have a chart here?" Dr. Staples frowned at the file, all business.

"I don't know," Margo said.

"You don't know? Well, have you brought him in to see us or not?" Do you know that?"

"No. I mean no we haven't been here before. But he may have. We recently adopted him. I found him at the Saturday market in Crystal Lake about a month ago. His owner died so he needed a new home. So I don't know if he has been here before. We never learned his name so we call him Roscoe. He doesn't seem to mind."

"I see," said the vet. "This is your first time coming to our practice, then?" He asked as he wrote a note in the file. "And Roscoe's first time - at least under this alias. Do you know the name of his previous owner?"

"Uh, yes. It was a Mrs. Whiting."

The vet turned to his receptionist who had seated herself again behind the desk and asked her to look up that name in their records. She plugged in the name and appeared to be reading down a list but shook her head when she got to the end. "No Whiting. Maybe she came from somewhere else, or maybe she just didn't take the cat in to see a vet."

"Thank you Vanessa. In that case we will have to make up a new file for Roscoe."

"Already started one, Dr. Staples." Vanessa clicked

open the screen she had been working on when she first sat down. Dr. Staples peered over her, pushing his glasses up and down, trying to get the best reading range. Vanessa seemed unfazed by the scrutiny and kept on entering the data she collected from Margo. She asked Margo a few preliminary questions like her full name, address, the possible age of the cat - between four and six years old Margo estimated.

"And the weight?" Dr. Staples asked that question, still trying to read it over her shoulder.

"He weighs 9.97 kilograms." Vanessa said.

The vet wrote that down and looked up. Pushing his glasses to the top of his nose, he said to Vanessa, "Almost 10 kilos! That's a fat cat! I think this is the fattest cat we ever had in our practice! Isn't that right, Vanessa?" Vanessa smiled a pitying smile towards Margo. Dr. Staples peered into the carrier and dictated a description of the cat for Vanessa to enter into the record: male adult, grey longhair domestic cat, obese.

Obese! Margo wanted to protest but the vet picked up the carrier and moved with precision into the room he had just exited. "Come with me, ma'am," he said brusquely.

Margo bristled at the reference to her as 'ma'am'. She said many times that this kind of nomenclature was out-of-date. Margo was of the opinion that men who called women 'ma'am' or referred to the female sex as 'ladies' and 'the fair sex' assumed women were helpless and clueless.

Dr. Staples was already pulling Roscoe out of his carrier and onto a shiny stainless steel table when Margo entered the examining room. He wasn't as gentle as Vanessa but then he didn't make horrific verbal bargains with him either.

"Shut the door behind you. Please and thank-you," he said without looking up. Roscoe tried to scrabble off the table, but the slippery surface gave him no purchase. Dr. Staples gripped him tightly with both hands around his waist. The hands, Margo noted, did not meet around Roscoe's circumference.

"Come over here and hold down his head and shoulders while I examine his anus," was the next command.

Margo did as she was directed. She wanted shut her eyes. Shouldn't this be the assistant's job? Apparently he and Vanessa didn't think so, so she was forced to watch Dr. Staples insert the thermometer. Roscoe let out a startled yowl.

When he had finished examining Roscoe from ears to anus, as he put it, he put him back into his carrier. "Roscoe checks out as a healthy neutered male cat. I doubt he has had his rabies and feline leukemia vaccines lately, so you might want to consider those as a precautionary measure even if he doesn't go out much."

"Can you take care of that today?" said Margo.

"Yes," the vet said, and made a note in the file, I'll do it now."

Margo held Roscoe firmly against her chest and stroked his head and under his chin, soothing him with promises of treats when he got home if he was a good boy. After carefully scrutinizing the labels while tipping his glasses up so he could see out of the lower part of the lenses, Dr. Staples shifted his focus to look over the top of his aviator glasses while he filled two syringes from two vials that he had removed from the shelf.

"Now ma'am, you will have to hold him down firmly so he doesn't scratch you while I administer these shots." He demonstrated how to hold Roscoe down on his side, with a forearm pressed into Roscoe's chest. From the wails and hisses Roscoe sent out, you would think he was being butchered. But Margo held him steady through two jabs. After that, Dr. Staples massaged Roscoe's rump and then his neck and ears, talking softly to him as if whispering to a horse. "Good job Fella. The pain will go away soon. You won't remember a thing."

"Finished." Dr. Staples' tone switched abruptly to the brusque, impersonal voice he used while talking to human clients. "You can put Roscoe back into his carrier now." He left Margo to shove a now, really pissed off Roscoe, back into his carrier and latch the door while the good doctor turned his back and paid attention to the safe disposal of the needles. After cleaning up and washing his hands, he turned around still drying his hands with a paper towel, and he looked over his aviator glasses at Margo.

"Roscoe is in good health for his age. I would say he is more like seven or eight years old by the look of his teeth. But the real threat to his health, ma'am, is his weight." Dr. Staples bunched up the paper towel and threw it into the disposal bin.

"Please call me Margo," Margo said. "Ma'am sounds too much like you are addressing my mother."

Dr. Staples blinked at her but didn't acknowledge her request. "How much do you feed him?"

"I keep his bowl full of dry food, so no set amount. Depends how hungry he is."

"That's wrong. You should control the food - not

the cat."

"But if his bowl is empty, he fusses and complains until I fill it."

"Ma'am," Dr. Staples began, "Margo, would you give in to your child if he threw a tantrum in a grocery store because he wanted a chocolate bar?"

"I don't have children," Margo said. "But I guess I wouldn't, no."

"So why do you give in to your cat?"

"Because he's a cat! And he's really annoying when he's hungry. I mean he just doesn't let up!" Margo was exasperated with this conversation. She knew where it was going and knew she wouldn't win.

"How long do you want Roscoe to live, Margo?" Dr. Staples asked - without looking at Margo. He had removed his glasses and began to polish them with a tissue he extracted with a quick tug from the dispenser on the counter.

"What kind of question is that? I guess as long as he is happy."

"He won't live long if you don't stop feeding him so much. And he won't have a happy life if he gets diabetes." Dr. Staples fitted his glasses onto his face and, with a middle finger, pushing them up to the bridge of his nose.

Did he just flip me the bird? Margo wondered for one second. *No, couldn't have. I'm sure he doesn't have that kind of rapport - or sense of humour, with his clients.*

"Does Roscoe have a regular regimen of activity?"

"Not unless you count walking to his bowl for a snack or walking to his litter box and then jumping back up onto the couch when he has completed his mission." The words just flipped out of Margo's mouth. She needed to do something to lighten the mood. She was starting to feel hot and claustrophobic in this little room.

"You need to take control of his diet and assist him in becoming more active if you want him to lose weight and live longer."

"But what can we do? He doesn't do anything all day. Just sleeps."

"Have ever you ever heard of play, Margo?"

Roscoe was getting restless in his carrier, waiting for the two humans to wrap things up. Finally, all patience at an end, he set up a tantrum of clawing at the metal hatch of his carrier.

Frustrated with what she thought was very poor client relations for a doctor, Margo waved her hand, motioning that this appointment was over. She picked up the carrier and almost sunk to her knees with the weight of it. "If that's all Dr. Staples, I'd like to take Roscoe and go home. It's a long drive."

"Fine," he said and looked at Margo without expression, "Please see my receptionist on the way out. She will write up the bill."

When Margo arrived home with Roscoe, she opened the door, shuffled in with the carrier and set it on the floor gently. "Here we are, Roscoe. Home sweet home. You can come out now." She said this in a low, singsong voice she hoped mimicked Vanessa's soothing style.

Roscoe didn't move right away. When he did, he nosed out carefully and sniffed the air before he set one paw out of his carrier. Then he stretched himself out to full length and headed straight to his food bowl.

When Margo swiftly picked up the bowl, Roscoe looked up at her in surprise and sleeked against her leg, purring. When his yowling campaign didn't work, this was his go-to behaviour.

Margo bent down and gave Roscoe a long stroke across his back. He returned her affection, sleeking against her leg and purring even louder.

Margo stroked his back and said in the same sweet voice, "I know what you're up to, big boy. You're just sucking up to me to get your way, aren't you?" She paused and looked down at Roscoe. He stopped sleeking and sat, glaring up at her. *I think he does understand me*, Margo thought. Raising her voice and adopting a firmer tone like a P.E. teacher she said, "I'm going to get you off that couch and you are going to exercise your lazy, entitled ass off!"

Suddenly Michael's head appeared over back of the couch. He had taken opportunity to catch a nap while the house was quiet and hadn't heard Margo and Roscoe come in. He blinked and then squinted.

"Huh? Margo? Are you talking to me?"

CHAPTER EIGHT

Major Tom to Ground Control

One of the first things Margo and Michael learned when they moved to Wannatoka Spring was that there were an unusual number of ATV vehicles used to commute around the village. Margo started recognizing the regulars who promenaded past their house by their sounds. A man who had hitched a trailer to his, loaded with leaves and branches, drove the one that sounded like it was missing a beat. An older man who had a hard time walking, drove by every day around two in a side-by-side with a small white dog barking from the passenger seat. She called the duo the 'town criers'. Their neighbours down the street made a slow-moving train; dad was on a quad with a youngster in his lap. Behind him on a smaller model, was the oldest boy, a teenager. Mom brought up the rear in her own quad. The family came out to take in the evening air - on four wheels. On one occasion while sitting on the porch swing reading on a sunny afternoon, Margo saw a couple race by on a newer model. Margo was certain they were traveling faster than an acceptable speed. Whether the purpose was to go into the bush to navigate the rough terrain on logging roads and trails, or as an easy commute to the neighbours' place, or just go for a joy ride, the ATV seemed to be the vehicle of choice for getting around in Wannatoka Springs.

Since he had seen his neighbours making use of their ATVs on the street to get to where they wanted to go, Michael thought he would imitate his neighbours by stopping by to visit when he went around the block and saw a neighbour outside working on his car in the drive-way or just sitting in a lawn chair smoking, watching their neighbours pass by and exchanging friendly salutations as they did. Half way down his street, Michael saw a neighbour working in his front lawn. He rolled up close to the fence and off the road.

"Hey John," Michael called out. John looked up.

"Oh, hey Michael, how's it going?" He pushed his cap back and swept his forehead with his forearm and then pushed his hat back down with the brim.

"Good! I see you're doing some work in your yard. If you need help with carrying those branches and debris to the burn pile, give me a shout. This thing's got a trailer I can hook up. Comes in handy." Michael patted the dash of his side-by proudly.

"That's a nice looking side-by you got there. Almost new." John said, "Looks like Leonard's. Did he sell it to you?"

Michael smiled proudly and turned off the engine. "Came with the house," he said, "We thought we could use it out here."

"Leonard hardly ever drove that thing," John said, "He took a couple of lessons from Ivan, and drove it to the burn pile a couple of times. But to be honest, I think he was scared of it. Just another city guy with money I guess, thinkin' he'd get a side-by to fit in and findin' out he couldn't tame the beast." John chuckled and spit on the ground to punctuate his point.

Michael tried not to look affronted. He stroked the steering wheel and replied, "Oh, I think I've got the hang of it. Been to the burn pile a couple of times. Thinking of taking the wife down to the beach next." Michael thought his use of 'the wife' made him sound local and experienced. He would never say that in front of Margo though.

"All good. Tons of sand to get stuck in!" John grinned. "So how are you settling in, anyway? I seen your wife sittin' on the porch swing when I passed by th'other day. Seems relaxed."

With that introductory query, Michael delved into their adventures starting with comparing notes on the evacuation. They agreed that a little more rain would be welcome to clear the air of smoke from the wildfires that were still raging across B.C. It had been a long drought and a poor harvest, especially since most of the gardens were left untended for a few weeks during the evacuation. John speculated on it being a long winter since they had such an extended summer. Talk moved on from the weather to what to expect of the Canucks this season. Michael wasn't a Canucks fan but he figured it was too early to express his opinion with the possibility of alienating his neighbour so he just went along with John's predictions for their chances this year.

Michael sat in the driver's seat throughout the conversation. From time to time, John leaned on his shovel and wiped his brow with the back of his hand, then repositioned his ball cap while he talked. When the conversation seemed to wane, Michael made his excuse to go on. "Well, gotta go check the mail. Should be sorted by now. Nice talking to you John!" he said, and started up his motor. John waved as he turned back to his shoveling.

That went well, Michael thought, as he drove cautiously down the street where they lived and rounded the corner to cruise down Maple Street. He didn't stop again, just waved at the neighbours who were out in their yards. The neighbours all returned friendly waves or a thumbs-up.

Michael's brief visit to the neighbour's on the side-by emboldened him. He thought he would use it more often just to get around. He might even sneak a couple of beer into his pockets and join the guys who regularly parked their ATVs on a neighbour's lawn down the street while they sat around drinking beer and shooting the bull. Margo wouldn't approve, but Michael figured she'd come around. It seemed to Michael to be the thing to do.

On a bright, sunny day, Michael decided to call his new friend, Joel. Joel and his wife, Tina, like Margo and Michael, were a retired couple who had just dis-covered Wannatoka Springs and bought a home just after Margo and Michael did. Their backyards butted up to each other, so they got to know each other first by chatting over the fence. Now Margo was going over to have coffee with Tina most mornings. Some mornings she would walk out in her pajamas and a light coat with her mug in her hand. She had to go all the way around the block because there was no gate between the two properties, but she didn't mind. Walking around the block to Tina's for coffee, Margo rationalized, seemed like a good start to her exercise routine.

In his chats over the fence with Joel, Michael found out that Joel liked to play a round of golf a few times a week. Michael said he was interested in golf, but hadn't played in a while. Work had kept him too busy. Joel said he would call him one day when he was going, to see if he wanted to come along.

On that particular day, Joel called Michael to ask if he would like to play a round of golf. Michael thought it would be an excellent idea. He told Joel he would pick him up in the side-by. They could throw their clubs in the back and drive out to the golf course, a nine-hole course across the highway. Joel agreed to meet Michael outside in front of their house in fifteen minutes.

When Michael told Margo, she surprised him by saying that she would go with him as far as Tina and Joel's place. Why not! It was a beautiful morning. It would be a lark driving down the street and around the corner to the neighbours, she said. She could visit with Tina while the boys went to play golf.

Michael and Margo traveled up their own street, turned down the connecting street, and were rounding the turn on to Maple Street when they saw their neighbour, Roger, out in his driveway talking with an RCMP officer. An RCMP car was parked on the street in front of his house. In their short time in Wannatoka Springs, neither Michael nor Margo had seen much of a presence of law enforcement. In fact, the only time they had seen an RCMP vehicle was when they were evacuated earlier that summer. At that time, the officer was directing traffic and blocking the entrance to the community so people could not re-enter or drive through it on their way to the ferry. Michael and Margo felt more secure leaving their property because of this visible show of the law. That single experience gave them the impression that the RCMP officers stationed in the hinterland were neighbourly and protective in a big brotherly sort of way. When Michael spotted the officer talking to Roger he slowed down and stopped in front of Roger's drive.

"Hi Roger!" Michael called out. "How's it going?" Margo smiled and waved, shouting her greeting to Roger from the passenger seat, "Beautiful morning!"

"Sure," Roger replied, "considering." He glanced at the officer and then down at something his toe was scraping off the asphalt.

"And good morning to you, officer," Michael said, offering him a friendly smile. "You visiting the neighbourhood?"

Margo leaned out to hear the conversation better and smiled her encouragement to the officer, waiting for his response. She thought she would interject that this was their first summer in this area and it was good to see the local RCMP taking an interest in their little community. But she didn't get the chance.

"No, I'm on official business."

For some reason, the presence of the officer on their neighbourhood street seemed to be a kind of cartoon in Margo's head.

"Oh!" She laughed, "Right! I see. You're wearing the official cop outfit!" Any presence of the law made Margo nervous. Even though she had never broken one in her life including going over the speed limit, she always felt like a criminal when she saw an officer of the law, even while she was walking on the street, and especially when an RCMP car drove behind her in traffic. When she got panicky she sometimes got silly and said things that were totally inappropriate for the situation. She winced. Outfit? She meant uniform. And what she really meant was that she could see by his uniform that this was official business, not just a friendly chat. But what came out sounded like it came out of the mouth of a giddy schoolgirl, not a composed, respected retired teacher of thirty-five years. Margo shifted her eyes away from the officer. She felt her face getting hot.

"I'm sorry officer," Michael said, trying to walk back the glib comment Margo made. "We were just passing by on our way to Tina and Joel's house and saw Roger out talking to you, so we thought we would introduce ourselves and let you know we are new to the neighbourhood." He smiled and then added, "Well, your business is not any of our business, so we'll be moving along,"

"Right," Margo said and smiled, "Sorry to interrupt."

But before Michael could ease off the brake and depress the gas pedal, the officer stepped towards

Michael and Margo, and in an officious tone said, "Do you have a 90 degree permit?"

Michael looked up, surprised. He hadn't thought he needed a permit to drive an ATV. "Uh, no. Not with me." He said, and then quickly added almost as a reflex, "I left it at home. I can go around the corner and get it if you want."

'Why did he say that?' Margo wondered. The previous owner had not left a license or instructions on how to get one. Did he think the officer would let that go?

The officer replied, "You need a variance permit to drive down a municipal street in an off-road vehicle. Otherwise it's illegal."

Margo, who was closer to the officer because she was in the passenger seat, said "Oh! Sorry about that! We didn't know because we just moved here."

The officer didn't look like he was going to let them go with that naive explanation.

"We were just coming to pick up Joel," Michael said, pointing down the street at Joel and Tina who were standing at the curb watching the interaction between Michael and the RCMP officer. "You see, our property butts against theirs, but there is a fence between us and we can't drive from our back yard to theirs because there is no gate, so we had to go around. It just seemed easier to take a vehicle, especially since we are going golfing." Michael seemed pleased with his reasoning. The officer looked above Michael's head.

"Where did you move from?" He asked, focusing again on Michael.

"Oh, Vancouver", Margo offered. "But we don't

have any experience with ATVs. This is the first one we have ever owned. It came with the house we bought, kind of an after thought. We really didn't want one, but the owner just threw it in with the house if we would agree to pay his full asking price. It's our first year, so we don't know the rules. Besides everyone else is doing it around here so we thought it was OK." She knew she was talking too fast and volunteering unnecessary information but that's the way she talked when she was nervous. Being in the presence of law enforcement always made Margo nervous. Even Officer Friendly, who came to the schools to have an informal chat with the kids made Margo nervous. While Officer Friendly was talking about obeying cross-walk signs, Margo was reviewing in her head if she had ever crossed before the light was flashing, and, if she had, if there had been any witnesses to her crime. This officer was clearly not Officer Friendly. While not impolite, his tone suggested he felt superior to the couple he was cautioning.

"The laws are the same all over the province," the officer replied patronizingly. If you have driven in BC you should know that. ATVs are off-road vehicles. I'm sure you don't see many in Vancouver and there's a reason for that. Do you know why that is?"

Margo shook her head slowly. She felt a lump form in her throat and her heart started pumping fast. She was sure she looked like the guilty teenager she had seen many times, slumped down in the chair in front of her teacher desk while she waved a paper in front of the student, explaining what plagiarism was and why it was a form of cheating - and that there is no excuse for claiming someone else's knowledge as your own.

The officer gave his answer without waiting for a reply, slowing the words down as if speaking to a young child who might not grasp the concept right away. "Because they are off-road vehicles. That means that they cannot be legally driven on municipal roads and highways." He stopped there and eyed both of them, waiting to see how they would respond. "But," he paused, "you can get a 90 degree permit. That would allow you to cross at a 90 degree angle to the road, say, from your property into the bush or onto an off-road trail."

Margo grinned and said "Thank you officer, Michael and I will drive to Crystal Lake tomorrow and apply for one. Where do we go to do that?"

The officer leaned on the roll bar and looked at Margo. "You apply with me. And I don't give them out." He said looking serious.

"So you are saying I can't go to the golf course with my buddy then?" Michael asked.

"Not if you have to come around the bend and go down this street to pick him up."

"I see," Michael nodded. He looked serious.

"I could give you a $625 ticket for driving an unlicensed vehicle on a municipal street and have it towed and impounded," the officer said. "You would have to pay another fee to get it out."

Margo gulped back a gasp. Her eyebrows shot up. The officer let that sink in for a beat and then said "But stopping you isn't why I'm here today so I'm letting you off with a warning."

Margo nodded and smiled. She hoped she had

recovered her responsible adult demeanour. "Thank you for the warning, officer . . . sorry, what was your name?"

"Tom" the officer said, "Corporal Tom Majors."

"Pleased to meet you, Corporal Majors" Margo smiled ingratiatingly. "I'm Margo and this is my husband Michael. We appreciate your guidance about the law." Michael cringed when he heard Margo say that. It sort of blew his cover of the cool new guy with ATV when his wife sounded like a nervous schoolgirl trying to earn brownie points. He was sure he'd never live it down with Roger anyway.

Not that Roger was listening closely. While the officer had engaged in this side-chat with Michael and Margo, Roger had gone back to the carport where his ex-wife was standing with their cat in her arms. She was loudly ordering him to get into his jeep and out of her sight so she and Mindy could get the hell out of there. It was her week to have her, she said, and she just might not bring her back. The cat was struggling to get out of her arms.

When Mindy buried a claw into the ex's neck in the struggle to get free, she lurch sideways and cursed it. Just then Officer Majors joined the couple as referee. She and the cat collided with the officer's chest and she lost her grip on the cat. The cat twisted out of her captor's arms and dug her claws into the officer's shirt, penetrating the cloth uniform in an effort to pull away from her abductor.

Michael drove towards Tina and Joel who were standing on their lawn, looking past them at the commotion on Roger's driveway. Joel had his clubs beside him. Tina had a cup of coffee in her hands. They looked on, amused at the sight of the officer wrestling with a cat trying to claw her way up to his shoulder to escape down his backside.

Michael drove up beside Joel and Tina and talked over the idling machine.

"What's going on?" Tina asked stretching her neck to see.

"I think it has something to do with Roger and his ex," Margo shouted over the idling engine. "We just came by and stopped to say a friendly 'hello', but it looks to me like Roger's ex called the cops on Roger. Seems like they're fighting over custody of the cat from what I can gather."

"Fun town!" Tina said and smiled into her cup as she took a sip of her coffee.

Margo smiled, 'Isn't it fun to be retired?"

With a backwards thumb over his shoulder Michael said, "Major Tom - back there - just told us that driving on the street is illegal. Who knew? We sure didn't. Anyway, I'm just going to drive it back around the block and park it and then walk back." Joel and Tina looked at each other and shrugged.

"Guess you'll know better next time, huh?" Joel said to Michael, and slapped him lightly on the upper arm. "If it were me, I'd have just waved and driven on down the road." He laughed and demonstrated a small wave just like the Queen on parade.

Margo climbed out of the side-by-side, and extracted her to-go cup filled with coffee from the cup holder. "I thought I'd just come over for a cuppa, Tina. Got time for a coffee?"

Tina smiled, "Sure! C'mon in!"

Margo was sitting on a stool at the island in Tina's kitchen, looking out at the front window when she saw Michael walking back, wheeling his golf cart behind him. Joel was still waiting for him in front of the house. When Michael got close, Joel rolled out with his golf cart and the two men walked down the middle of Maple Street. The only 90 degree crossing today would be walking across the highway to the golf course on the other side.

When she reviewed that story later, Margo thought *I wonder if this incident will trigger a sting operation in Wannatoka Springs. I can just see Major Tom (that was his nick name forevermore) driving up and down one of the five streets, or laying in wait around the bends for any ATVs, golf carts, and lawn tractors that might be driving on one the five streets with the intention of restoring law and order to this lawless community in the hinterland.*

If the operation were to be a success, Margo thought, *the sting would have to be planned for either the 10 a.m. meeting at the post boxes, or the 3 p.m. happy hour at any one of the neighbours houses - the daily Wannatoka Springs rush minute.*

Margo giggled to herself at a new article that flashed into her mind - *retired actuary and teacher, Michael and Margo (AKA Bonny and Clyde) were chased by RCMP officer, Major Tom, who followed closely on their ATV bumper until they make a 90 degree turn onto an open field. Wheeling in wide slow circles around the field, they eluded Major Tom who was forced (by law) to stick to the municipal roads that border the field. He called out on his loud speak, "Turn yourselves in. We WILL find you. There is no escape from the law - even in Wannatoka Springs."*

CHAPTER NINE

Living the Dream: Michael Joins the Fire Brigade

One fall morning, Michal walked through the front door of the house they had newly settled into, and called out for Margo. The timbre of his voice betrayed his excitement.

"In here," Margo called back, not looking up from what she was reading. She was sitting in her recliner, the matching one to Michael's which was parked parallel to hers. They had brought them from their home in the city and set them up in the living room facing the windows overlooking their backyard and the backyards of their neighbours. Above the roofs of their neighbours' houses, they could gaze at the forested hills on the other side of the lake that appeared as a sliver of water threading through mature trees in front.

"You will never guess what I've done," Michael said, wearing a self-satisfied smile.

Margo looked up from her reading and tilted her glasses down her nose so she could meet her husband's eyes with clarity. "No I probably won't. So, you had better just tell me." Michael was too impatient to wait for her to guess, anyway. He looked like a little boy bursting with news. "I just signed up with the Wannatoka Springs volunteer fire brigade!" He puffed out his chest and pointed at himself with his thumb. "Can you believe that? At age sixty-five, I am finally going to be able to fulfill my childhood dream of becoming a fireman."

Margo smiled and cocked her head to one side. "I didn't know that was your childhood dream. But then, who dreams to become a number cruncher at eight years old. And you found something to do in your retirement. Good for you! When do you start this new occupation?"

One of the first things Margo and Michael said they would do when they retired was to look for something that would help them redefine and shape the meaning of this new stage in their lives. Margo had read this advice in one of the books she started collecting on the subject of preparing for retirement. The literature suggested that some retirees join clubs whose interests appeal to them. Michael didn't resent his choice of careers, and he was very successful, but being successful meant making sacrifices so he never joined clubs or recreational teams.

Being childless, both Margo and Michael spent their whole adult building their careers. Neither of them felt the loss of a hobby or recreation, but they did see that they would need to do something or join something to fill the void in retirement. Furthermore, their careers had always defined who they were. At a social gathering, for example, if Michael or Margo met someone new and were asked introductory questions, the first would likely be 'What do you do?" Michael's answer was, "I'm an Insurance Actuary." That often left the other person at a loss because they had no idea what an insurance actuary did. So, the other person might say, "How interesting. Where do you work?" The answer was straightforward as Michael worked in an office on Burrard St. in downtown Vancouver.

The conversation might then drift to the other's experience of seeing, or walking past the business district, noting the architecture or discussing unfortunate increase of the homeless who were camping around there, having to walk around them on their way, not feeling safe in that area anymore and so on. Or they might segue into their career choice to fill the void.

The odd person might ask a question they might later regret, like "Oh? What does an Insurance Actuary do?" This would allow Michael, who rarely had a chance to explain the role of the actuary, an opportunity to introduce the nature of how essential it is to the business. His unwittingly captive audience would learn about analysis, the financial costs of risk and uncertainty, and statistics. If given enough time before the other person politely excused themselves, he could explain the financial theory and probability assessment of the risk incurred.

The actuary's calculations determined the company's insurance program. It was all about the odds being in favour of the house, Michael said, making a gambling allusion intentional so the other person could relate.

Often, as Michael wound up his inevitably long-winded lecture on a topic he was passionate about, the eyes of the person he had engaged were skating around the room looking for an escape. If he did get a chance to finish to the end, he always told the same joke.

"What did God say when he created actuaries? 'Go figure!' And the actuaries took it literally." Michael always laughed at the punch line and repeated it. "Go figure." His audience would smile politely or even evoke a chuckle, but odds were they'd walk away wondering what the joke was. In the middle of the night they might wake up and get it though.

Margo was a high school English teacher. And reactions she endured were often a light-hearted ribbing. "Remind me not to send you an email. I wouldn't want to be corrected by an English teacher," or "Better mind my p's and q's around you!" The worst responses she was forced to listen to were the ones where the other person described their terrible experience in high school (especially in English) and how, to this day, having been so traumatized by their English teacher, they loathed reading and hated writing. Some admired her for being on the 'front lines' of education. Teaching high school was not something they could ever see themselves doing, 'but kudos to you!'

Both Michael and Margo found satisfaction in their careers, and pride in how they built their reputations and won the respect of their colleagues through their advancement. Now that they were retired though, they both felt as if, suddenly, their identities had been ripped off and thrown away like a name-tag worn at a convention. Being 'retired' seemed so static and open-ended. Your identity was linked to what you did, and not so much to who you are now.

Margo had yet to find an immersive hobby or activity. She liked photographing sunsets and other natural vistas, with her camera. And she blogged her journey from the city to the Kootenays. The journey itself was a novelty. She posted it for her friends. Scrolling through their comments, and the names of the people who 'liked' her posts kept alive her connections to friends she had left behind when she moved. But that activity had its limitations. She really didn't know what she wanted to do or what would give her meaning in this phase of her life. Not wanting to think about it too much, she would pick up a book and settle down in her recliner.

Michael had just come in from his walk to the post boxes. The same group of men gathered there most mornings, talking while waiting for their mail to arrive. The subject came up about the fire that summer and the evacuation order. Since then, there had been a renewed interest in building up the volunteer fire brigade, which had dwindled to three or four members. The scare of a wildfire coming close enough to a tiny community surrounded by forest had renewed a sense of urgency to revive the brigade.

This struck a chord with Michael. He was excited about attending his first fire hall training meeting. He also thought he would use this opportunity to use the ATV as a convenient commuter vehicle, something he had seen so many of the other men doing.

He just fired up the ATV in the backyard and left it idling while he walked toward the gate to open it so he could drive it onto the street, when Margo popped her head out the back door. She thought she heard the ATV and wondered what Michael was up to this time of evening. He said he was going to fire brigade practice. She hoped he didn't think he was going to drive it there. She didn't like taking chances and was especially nervous about breaking the law. "You aren't going to take that thing to the fire hall are you Michael?"

"What?" Michael cupped his ear as if he couldn't quite make out what Margo was saying.

"The fire hall. Practice tonight. You aren't driving there in the ATV are you?" She kept her sentences deliberately short so her words would be clear over the motor's loud rattle.

Michael nodded and waved. "Taking her to the fire hall. See you after practice!" He stepped one foot on the gas, easing it forward. The engine revved even louder. Margo tried to gesture her concern, waving her arms, cutting her throat, making a 'T' with her hands. But Michael seemed not to understand any of her signals. She stopped short of standing in front of it, using her body as a human shield to block his path. Finally giving up her protest, her arms hanging limp at her sides, Margo watched Michael's back as he chugged down the street.

The fire hall was ablaze with lights and buzzing with eager recruits, both men and women, of a wide age range from teens to folks in their early seventies - who were also excited about joining the fire brigade that Tuesday evening. Kyle, the fire chief, looked around scrutinizing the crowd - nineteen including three of the old guard and sixteen uninitiated. Kyle called for order. "Lets get this meeting started. First off, you will all need to find a place on one of the benches on either side of the hall. Next, I'll call role. You answer if you're here. And if I get your name wrong, you can correct me." Having gone through that, he started to explain the role of the volunteer fire department. The eager newbies leaned in to catch every word he was saying.

"We all pray that there won't be a repeat of last year's fire season," Kyle went on. Everyone murmured assent. "If there is, however, or even a domestic event, volunteers will need to be proficient in all matters of operating the fire trucks as well as handling the equipment and executing the necessary steps to prevent further damage." Everyone nodded and listened.

Kyle's first day review included the rules and expectations of volunteer fire department. A domestic fire can be fought from the outside of the building. So any indoor fire hazards in the kitchen like grease fires from leaving the bacon to burn in the frying pan, or letting a candle burn down and catch the sheets on fire during feverish bedroom exercises, were discouraged. Kyle paused there, and stroked his full reddish beard, waiting for a tittering response and then went on.

"If such potentially hazardous activities are engaged in by the members of the public, remember the WFSB is not qualified to run into any burning buildings to save your lit ass." Kyle said and paused for a reaction. A round of titters escaped from the newbies. The long-time members just rolled their eyes. They had heard Kyle's lines before. Michael made a mental note to find out what 'lit' meant in this case. He would ask Margo to Google it when he got home.

After his speech, Kyle handed out the gear- an assortment of nearly worn out, and damaged hand-me-downs. There was a pile of flame-retardant jackets and another of pants. For the next half hour or so the fire hall's discipline unraveled. Everyone rummaged through the two piles trying on and tossing gear back onto the piles in an effort to find something that fit, somewhat.

Kyle remained on the sidelines taking notes. Some couldn't find pants and others couldn't find jackets. Some boots were not in their sizes and gloves had holes in them or were not a matching pair. The fact was, the fire department had been allowed to deteriorate over the years as the attrition of volunteers had depleted and resources had dried up and it was almost to the point of being non-functioning.

Kyle penciled notes in his scribbler beside the name of each person who couldn't find suitable gear, patiently asking the participant what their size was and promising to order replacements as soon as their budget allowed - which, he emphasized, would depend on their fundraising efforts he would address in future meetings.

When the scuffed yellow fire fighter helmets were passed around, Michael looked at his and turned it over in his hands. Misty with nostalgia, he pictured his eight-year-old self, running around the house calling, "Fire!"

His mom hadn't appreciated that startling announcement at first. But by the time he reached an age where he didn't play fireman anymore, and she had to pack his fireman paraphernalia away with his other outgrown favourite toys, she felt sentimental about her boy growing up so fast.

Michael struggled into a pair of pants to find a gaping hole in the shin. That's not safe, he thought. The fire could potentially burn right through to the skin. When he pointed this out to Kyle, he was told that a new pair would be ordered but he should wear them for now, just to get the feel for the gear. Michael duly went along with this idea but secretly worried he might have to actually attend a fire with ripped pants. He wondered if Margo could sew the gap up if he managed to sneak them out of the hall.

When the group had sorted out which gear fit best, they stood together, forming a motley crew dressed in over-sized or undersized jackets that were missing clasps, pockets flapping off at the seams, suspendered pants that were too long, or too short, or ripped in the knee or down a seam in the seat. Kyle inspected the crew and said, "Gear will be replaced as we can afford to replace it. Meantime, this gear is good enough to practice with."

Kyle then announced that they would all take a ride around the block on the two fire trucks parked outside, just to get a feel for it. He and, assistant chief Cam and Eddie would be the drivers. There was a buzz of muted excitement in the interchanges among the new recruits. Over the next five minutes, Kyle assigned personnel to the trucks. Michael and Joel climbed into the red fire truck, a 1969 relic that had to be babied to start - an effort that sometimes took up to twenty minutes. That was time enough for a fire to burn down a building, Michael noted later when he told Margo about his adventure.

Once on the road the two trucks made an impressive convoy, the first responder truck in the lead, the newer model yellow truck next and the old, red truck bringing up the rear. Michael was ecstatic! He gripped the bar on the back with both hands and looked around at his neighbourhood from his vantage point, high up, almost level with the roofs. And when Cam turned on the siren briefly, Michael let out a whoop just like a kid. Grinning, Michael turned to Joel who was beside him. Joel was holding on to the bar with one hand and his hat with the other. His fire helmet was too big for his head and he hadn't learned yet how to adjust it, so when he twisted his head around, the helmet wobbled over his eyes. Joel had an equally wide grin on his face. "This is so cool!" Joel shouted above the siren's wail. Michael nodded and faced front again. He never even dreamed he would get to ride on a fire truck, but as luck would have it, here he was . . . training for a new role as a volunteer fire fighter!

Returning to the station, they carefully dismounted the trucks and talked excitedly about their experience. Kyle shouted above the din and whistled for their silence. All eyes turned towards their leader. "Glad you all had fun," Kyle started, "but remember, this is serious business. And there's a lot to learn before you will be of use in an actual fire - God forbid. Now . . . that's enough for this evening. Thank you for coming out. I hope to see you all here again next Tuesday." He instructed the crew to remove their turnout gear, stow and hang it up in their assigned places.

Michael hung his jacket on the hook in front of him. Next he stripped off his pants. As he tried to do this, he got stuck and hopped around, then sat down hard on the bench. He hadn't thought to take off his boots first. He laughed at his mistake and carried on. Joel, who was watching and copying Michael's method, learned quickly from Michael's mistake and sat down to unbuckle his boots before he tried to get his pants off. They kicked the boots off, then stripped off the pants they had put over their jeans, a task that was no mean feat. When that was accomplished, they stood in front of their places on the bench and folded the heavy, waterproof overalls neatly into thirds and placed them on the bench, helmets rested on the pants. Not sure where to put their boots, they placed them under the bench and stuffed the gloves into a boot so they wouldn't get lost. Their two piles of gear looked like they had been arranged with military precision.

Kyle came by to inspect. He studied the neatly folded pants and the boots paired under the bench with gloves stuffed inside. "Very neatly done! But this isn't Home Economics ladies!"

As Kyle stressed the word 'ladies', a smile twitched like an electric current through his beard for a split second. "What if there was a fire?" He frowned, "You would have to unfold your pants then shake them out while you danced across the floor trying to get them on one leg at a time. And, assuming you put your gloves on first when you pulled them out of your boots, you would have to removed your gloves because your hands wouldn't fit through the sleeves of the jacket. By the time you were suited up, the rest of us would have been half way down the block in the fire truck." He stroked his beard and shook his head. Michael and Joel looked down at their neat stacks and then at each other. "Here let's show you how it's done." He called Cam, who was still suited up, to come over to them and explained that these ladies clearly knew how to fold laundry but didn't know how to get out of their gear so they could get it on fast. Cam smiled, but he didn't say anything. He respectfully demonstrated how to take off the gear so that he would literally be able to jump into it in a hurry. First he loosened off his boots, but didn't take them off. Then he stripped down his pants so they were scrunched over his boot bottoms and sat down, carefully pulling his feet out without dislodging the pants that remained over them. He stepped out of the gear leaving the pants rolled over the boots, then hung the jacket on the bottom hook, shoving the gloves into the pockets and hung his helmet on the top hook.

"Now that's how you do it," Kyle said nodding approval at Cam. "That way when you go to get dressed you just have to jump into your pants and boots in one slick motion, put your jacket on, secure the clasps, grab your gloves and your hat and you're good to go." Kyle thanked Cam who gathered up his gear and went over to his spot.

When they dismissed for the night, Michael and Joel walked out of the hall and Joel imitated Kyle's address.

"Good work ladies, but this isn't Home Economics!" They both sniggered. When he saw Kyle and Cam emerge from the hall Joel waved. "Good night from the ladies!" Cam grinned and gave them the thumbs up. Kyle shook his head and stroked his beard. Michael told Joel he could hardly wait until they learned to drive the truck - and that night's antics cemented their friendship. They said goodnight and walked away from the hall in the opposite directions, heading back to their houses.

Michael walked almost half way home when he realized he had driven the side-by to the practice. He smacked his forehead and shook his head, smiling to himself as he walked back to retrieve it. He was relieved to see that the lights were turned off and that no one was lingering outside the hall when he returned. For some reason he felt sheepish that he had forgotten to fire up his ATV and drive away like everyone else. Opening the front door, he called out to Margo.

"I'm here," Margo called from the living room, not looking up from her book.

"This is going to be so much fun!" Michael shouted. Still feeling pumped, he talked quickly and gestured dramatically. "Tonight we got to put on the turn-out gear and I got my own suit. The pants have a rip in the knee. I'm hoping you can fix them. Kyle said he would order new ones eventually, so it would just be for practice. And I folded up the gear instead of just jumping out of it. So Kyle called Joel and I out for not having put away our gear in the right order. Apparently we both got it wrong. So Kyle comes over and says, "Nice job, ladies! But this isn't Home Economics!"

Margo stared at Michael over her reading glasses,

wondering what had happened to transform her husband from a serious professional to a laughing, gesturing . . . boy!

"And we got to ride the fire truck! A real old-fashioned red fire truck where you can actually stand up behind the cab, feeling the wind in your face. And next week," Michael said, taking in a breath, "Kyle - that's the fire chief - said Joel and I are going to learn how to drive it!"

Margo nodded and watched Michael hotfooting around the room explaining his adventure. When it appeared to her that he had spit out the whole story, she smiled and said, "I'm glad you boys had fun!"

After that, every time Michael went out the door on Tuesday nights to go to fire practice, he fired up the side-by and trundled down the street to the fire hall. As he left the house, Margo called after him "Have fun!" And every evening after he came home from fire practice, Michael came in the house with glint in his eye and the same boyish grin on his face. Margo would invariably ask, "So? Did you have fun? What did you do?" That was Michael's cue to recount to Margo what had been on the fire practice agenda that night.

Michael was living the dream. Not the dream of retirement per se, but the long ago dream of an eight-year-old boy. Even if it was just for the couple of hours he spent with the Wannatoka Springs Volunteer Fire Brigade on Tuesday nights.

CHAPTER TEN

Is That a Deer Hanging In The Neighbour's Carport?

It was a crisp, sunny, November day. Margo and Michael walked Chance around the block and down Maple Street. The now mature maple, chestnut and spruce trees linking the street were planted in the 1960s when the community was purpose-built by the hydro company which had appropriated and then flooded the valley of rich farmland and orchards to create a lake, a reservoir really, that would feed water into the hydro-electric dam miles away. Most of the homes were unremarkable, one story, boxes built with economy, not architectural flair, in mind. Some were converted or built over double-wide trailers. Some had carports or additions built later. But what almost all of them had was a front porch. On a fine day like this, neighbours could be seen drinking coffee in the morning and beer in the afternoon. When Margo and Michael passed by, one couple called out to ask if they would like a cup of coffee - or a beer. Their choice. "Thanks, maybe next time," Michael said, waving. "Enjoy the day! Especially the sunshine!" The couple raised their mugs in salute.

Having friendly neighbours was one of the reasons Margo and Michael felt good about their decision to retire to this tiny community, despite the unfamiliarity of some of the norms and customs of the small village Kootenay culture. One of those established customs was hunting. Both men and women bought hunting licenses at the beginning of the season and set out to stock up on their meat for the winter. This was the start of week one of deer hunting season. The topic of the porch banter these days was all about hunting. Having nothing relevant or acceptable to contribute to those conversations, Margo and Michael often declined invitations to join in the impromptu porch stories of how the hunter stalked his target, or bragged about the number of points on the antlers of their kill. Apparently, the more there were, the more impressive the animal, thus the more impressive the hunter's prowess.

As they walked down the sidewalk, the local pot grower, Spliff, passed them on his ATV. He slowly made his way down the street, stopped just ahead of them and drove onto the lawn where a man was sitting on his porch drinking a beer.

"Hello Buckaroo!" Spliff called out over the running motor. "Have you bagged your deer yet?" Spliff was a fixture in Wannatoka Springs. He raised and sold marijuana plants. He could be seen driving around in his side-by with a delivery of starters for local gardeners and often stopped to shoot the bull with anyone who happened to be out on their porch and gave him the time of day -

which was nearly every one. Not only was Spliff a fountain of information on marajuana, he was also the local gossip and knew what was happening or why it wasn't happening, as well as the government's intentions for and interference with this rural community. And, he was funny. No one could lead you down a garden path like Spliff - and leave you at the gate, scratching your head, trying to figure out how you could have been so sucked in by his story. When he saw the look that told him his audience had realized their gullibility, he chortled at his own hyperbole.

"Nope. Not yet," said Buck. "Went out th'other day. Seen a six pointer. But it scared off before I could get a clear shot. My phone went off. Can you believe it? In the middle of the woods!"

Spliff laughed. And that started a sputtering cough, a tell of his long-time smoking habit. When he cleared his throat, he said, "So, what was so urgent? Win the lottery?" He guffawed.

"The wife wanted to know when I would be home for dinner."

Spliff took a drag on the cigarette he held between his thumb and forefinger, sheltered in the palm of his hand. Then he leaned over as if to give Buck confidential advice, shouting it, nevertheless, from the street to the porch where Buck was sitting. "Did ya tell her that you'd be late now that she scared off dinner?"

Buck let out a sharp "Ha!" and pointed at Spliff. "Good one!"

Spliff waved and moved on slowly down the street, smoke trailing as if he was an engineer driving a train. He was heading down the street to call on another neighbour where he could tell them the story - with his punch line. It WAS a good one.

Margo and Michael had heard the exchange. They looked at each other and smiled at the joke. When they came to Buck's porch, Michael called out "Hi, Buckaroo!"- trying to imitate Spliff's easy-going salutation. "Heard you didn't bag your deer." Michael didn't know exactly what it meant to bag a deer. He used the term only because he heard Spliff use it and thought it would make him sound more 'in the know'.

"Hey, Michael. No I didn't. And it's Buck."

"Oh - sorry, Buck, I thought I heard Spliff call you that."

"Ach, he does. The old coot!" Buck spit on the ground. "But he's the only one. We got history. Anyway, don't matter. Call me what you want. Just so you don't call me late for dinner!" Buck grinned and winked at Michael. Michael smiled. Margo was looking off into the middle distance trying not to laugh at that old cliché. "Huntin' season's just started. I'll get that old sonofagun! Just you wait. You hunt, Michael?" Buck lit the joint he was holding and drew in a drag.

"Oh, no. Not me." Michael demurred. "I grew up in the city. All we hunted for were bargains in the super-market." Michael grinned. Buck coughed out the smoke. Margo thought Michael's joke was lame but then, so was Buck's. She smiled in solidarity.

"Yup. The wife does that. She seen a sale on ham-burger in the flyer th'other day and drove to Crystal Lake to scoop up the deal. I told her, when she got home, that she probably spent the money she saved on the gas just gettin' there. There's no such thing as a bargain anymore, no matter what them sales flyers tell ya. Just jack up the prices so they can put them on sale. That's why I hunt. A deer or a moose in the freezer goes a long way. It'll carry us through the winter and then some."

"Good point!" Michael agreed. "Well, good luck with catching a deer then," he said, and waved indicating they were moving on. Margo grimaced when Michael said 'catching' a deer. Even she knew you shot or bagged a deer. She made a mental note to 'catch' Michael up to speed on hunting lingo.

Buck seemed oblivious to Michael's comment, though. He took a hit off his joint, held it in for a moment or two, exhaled and said, "Have a good evening you two."

Michael took Margo's hand and the two of them walked the rest of the way up Maple Street and rounded the corner where the fire hall was located, waving at the Fire Chief. The old red fire truck was parked out in the drive. The chief waved back with a spanner in his hand and then ducked under the hood. After that, he could only been seen from behind. Margo didn't want to say so, but she recognized that butt.

They turned the corner again onto their street. Neighbours who were out in their yards raking leaves or sitting on their porch waved and smiled or called out a friendly "hello" as they walked by.

"Such a peaceful, place," Margo said when they came to their house. "What a change from the city."

"The biggest change is being able to walk down the street and not compete with cars. No traffic," Michael added. "No road rage, no honking, no construction."

Just as Michal finished his litany, a cacophony of loud voices hurling insults and accusations at each other pricked the silence like balloons suddenly being popped one after the other. Their neighbours were fighting on their porch again.

"Well, not perfectly peaceful." Margo sighed, "Ivan and Brittany going at it again. I guess every neighbourhood has its flaws."

"Paper walls." Michael reminded Margo with a smile.

"We are new here." Michael said, "Remember the Prime Directive from Star Trek?" Michael referenced his favourite cult sci-fi show's premise. "When encountering a new civilization, there must be no interference with the normal development of the society."

Margo rolled her eyes, but was happy to go into their house and shut out the angry exchange. It felt like the neighbours across the street thought their porch was their living room. Margo didn't like sitting on her porch across from them when they argued. She didn't share Michael's love of Star Trek or his philosophy of the prime directive - but she did see his point. They were not in their element here. She needed to be more of an observer and less judgmental about what her neighbours did in their all-to-public private spaces. Still she did appreciate that, when she closed her front door, she didn't have to look at or listen to anything she didn't want to see or hear.

She made a cup of tea and sat down in her favourite lounge chair and gazed out at her neighbourhood, laid out in front of her from her out-sized living room windows. From her perch, she could look down onto the houses whose backyards met theirs, and see between the houses, stretches of Maple Street. There was Joel, walking his dog. And out in front of their porch Evelyn, Buck's wife, had just joined Buck. Margo smiled to herself when she saw Buck take another drag from his joint and thought about Michael's gaff, 'good luck catching your deer'. She wondered how many missteps she might have made without knowing it while trying to fit in.

Neighbours here didn't seem to want to correct you too much, unless it was something important to them like being addressed by their preferred name - Buck, not Buckaroo for instance. Margo laughed at the image that came to mind when she heard the word *Buckaroo* in her head. A cowboy riding a fast horse through a sagebrush desert to catch the train robber, sprang to mind. Stooped, skinny, with rheumy eyes from chain-smoking pot, Buck did not resemble any hunky cowboy she had seen in westerns when she was a kid, but maybe he did once. And maybe that was the history between Buck and Spliff - young bucks riding high on adventures to the tune of 'spare the horse and ride a cowboy'.

Swiveling in her chair, Margo watched the next-door neighbour's boy rake their backyard of newly fallen leaves. *He was a good boy*, she thought. He always seemed to be cooperative with his parents, and he greeted Margo politely when she walked by. The young family had moved in to the house next door late last summer, soon after Margo and Michael settled. They had come from northern B.C. The wife, Vanessa, said she had grown up in the area. Her parents lived in Crystal Lake. She had her own home-based business which she described as selling vitamin supplements and natural health improvement products - 'helping people take charge of their health the way God intended - through holistic products that would boost your own natural defenses'. Her husband, Blake, was a heavy-duty mechanic and worked in a machine shop just this side of Crystal Lake. They had one son, eleven-year-old Isaiah. He was a quiet, solitary kid. Maybe because he had just started school in September, he wasn't bringing home friends yet. When he wasn't by himself, he was helping his mother with the lawn and garden. *Friendships would come,* Margo thought. It took some kids more time to develop friendships than others.

Margo heard Vanessa call to her son to come and help her with something. Indifferently, Margo tracked the son's path. He let the rake fall where he had started the pile and walked nonchalantly towards his mom who was standing at the edge of the carport. Something caught her eye. She sat straight up and strained to make sense of what she was seeing. A knife-edge glinted off the sunlight. Was that a butcher knife Vanessa was holding? What was Vanessa doing with a butcher knife? Margo hoped she wasn't going to witness a crime. She didn't want to get involved, but if it affected a child it was her responsibility. Margo stood up and walked to the side window to get a closer look, but couldn't quite make sense of what she saw.

What was hanging behind Vanessa? A body? Whatever it was, it looked like it was hanging upside down from the rafters of the carport. Margo's eyes widened. She covered her gaping mouth to stifle the urge to scream. It was as long as a human adult, but it didn't look human. It had four legs. The back two legs were trussed together and a thick rope bound them together and hooked into a chain. It looked like an upside down trope of a teller reaching for the sky when the bank robber says, "this is a stick-up!" When she followed the body down to the floor, she recognized the head of a deer. It's antlers scraped the floor and it's tongue lolled loosely from an open mouth. The dead deer rotated slightly on its hook and Margo stepped back, horrified. She grabbed her binoculars and sat back down in her chair, waiting to see what would happen next.

What happened next was something Margo had never seen before, not even on nature shows. When she recognized what she was looking at, she let out a gasp and nearly dropped the binoculars.

"Michael!" she called out frantically. Her heart pulsed in her chest. "Michael? Michael! If you can hear me . . . come up here!"

"Coming, Love!" Michael called back from the depths of his room in the basement.

Margo heard him taking the stairs two at a time. He had been in his 'man-cave', as he called the room he claimed downstairs, sorting out his albums into alphabetical order and screening those he no longer wanted to keep. He had collected vinyl albums since he was young and had an impressive collection of classic rock dating back to the original albums of the Beatles era. He hadn't heard Margo so much as felt the vibration of her screeching call. She had shrieked like a trapped animal and an alarm tripped in his head and he charged up the stairs with no other thought than - *Margo's in trouble!*

Margo stood, nearly frozen with fright, the binoculars swinging from her hand by the strap. Avoiding staring out the window, she pointed dumbly to the scene below it. "Michael, look out the window and tell me what you see. No. Wait. Don't." Margo held her hands up to stop Michael from coming any closer. "I'll tell you what you will see. I think there's a dead deer hanging in our neighbour's carport."

Michael raised his eyebrows and moved toward the window, hands on hips and peered out at the scene in the neighbour's yard and carport below. Margo pulled her eyes away and stood by, refusing to look down until Michael came up to join her. The other member of the family, the father, Blake, had joined the tableau. Michael saw the deer. It was partially obscured by the three figures that surrounded it, mom, dad and son all with sharp knives, cutting away. Long swaths of hide were already on the floor exposing the raw, meaty bones and flesh beneath. Their hands were covered in blood as they slashed through the hide, and at times, ripped it downward, slicing and tearing it as they went.

"What the . . .? Wait! Can't quite make out what's going on." Michael moved in one direction and then the other, trying to see past the backs of the family in front of the hanging carcass. "Hand me the binoculars, Margo!" Michael snapped. Margo weakly handed them over, still averting her eyes.

"Do you see what those people are doing?" Margo's voice squeaked out.

Michael was fascinated with what he was witnessing, but he toned down his enthusiasm because he saw the effect it had on Margo. "Yes. Looks like they caught their deer," he said.

"Bagged their deer," Margo's muffled correction came out from behind her hand that still covered her mouth. "And now they're butchering it!"

"OK. Bagged their deer. And now they're dressing it." Michael corrected. Without taking his binoculars off the scene down below. "I heard Buck telling the guys a story once about dressing his deer in the field where he shot it. I think that means skin it, and cut it up before they haul it back home. Just the hunks that they can butcher later. The torso and haunches meat. No legs, or guts and stuff. Antlers if they want to keep them as trophy."

Margo swallowed the bile that rose in her throat. "Dressing it?" She said faintly? "More like undressing it." She smiled at her own joke and relaxed her mouth and her hands a little. But she still wasn't willing to look out the window. "Dressing the deer. Wonder what backwards wood-chopper thought that one up."

Margo closed her eyes, stretched out one of her arms, and struck a pose with an imaginary knife swiping in a slow downward motion. As she pantomimed the young wife's deft movements, she said, "You should have seen Vanessa wield that knife. She's teaching her son to butcher too! Nice home schooling lesson!" Margo opened her eyes and went on, using her mock teacher voice, the voice she used when she joked about the funny things teachers said or did in the name of education. "Today students, we are going to learn how to dress a deer. Or should that be undress a deer? This will count for a an assignment in your grade eight foraging class. So put down your pencils and pick up your sharpest knife."

"I'm sure they know what they are doing," Michael said, turning back to view the operation. For a minute he felt like he was standing behind the glass in a surgical theatre, observing the surgeon run his scalpel deftly through the patient's body, with the nurses standing at the ready to hand him the tools and sponges. He put down the binoculars and shrugged. "I suppose it's a valuable skill out here in the hinterland - not to mention the savings on meat. Like Buck said, meat's not cheap any way you cut it. That's why he hunts he said, to fill his freezer for the winter."

Margo's hands were tingling. The feeling was coming back to them and her heart had stopped racing. She took a breath and lifted up her hair, airing out her neck, damp with sweat. She was surprised at her physical reaction to the sight. "When that blood came spurting out of the neck, I just . . ." her voice trailed off. "Never mind. I'll make myself a cup of chamomile tea and take a breath."

"Here, sit down, " Michael held her shoulders firmly with both hands and guided her to her chair and then drew the drapes on the side window closed. "You just put your feet up and relax. Take a few deep breaths. I'll make you a cup of tea."

Margo closed her eyes and stretched her arms up over her head, then brought them together palms pressed towards each other in a prayer. She breathed in deeply. As she exhaled, she brought her praying hands to her chest. She repeated this three times before she opened her eyes. By the time she had gone through her seated yoga breathing, Michael had made her a cup of tea and put it in her hand. She clasped the warm cup and looked out through the windows in front of her at her own serene backyard and the tops of the roofs of the neighbours' houses on Maple Street. With the side curtain pulled, the scene in the neighbour's carport had vanished.

"You're right, Michael," she said. "It's like we are exploring another world or civilization."

When she was calmer, she went to the kitchen to decide what she should make for dinner. She thought she would make a vegetarian lasagna. In the aftermath of what she had witnessed that afternoon, she toyed with the idea of becoming a vegetarian as she layered the pasta with the tomato sauce, ricotta, spinach and cheese - but she filed that thought into the 'to think about later' folder.

The next day, on their walk, Michael and Margo saw their next-door neighbour in the front yard with her son. They were raking leaves into a pile. "Good morning!" Michael called out cheerily. "Beautiful fall day, isn't it!" Vanessa looked up from her work and shaded her eyes. Recognizing her neighbours, she smiled and said, "It is! Good day for starting fall clean-up!"

"They sure pile up!" Margo tried out her voice, going for nonchalant and conversational, hoping it didn't give away her shock at seeing this same woman yesterday sawing off the head of a deer.

"They do! I can't wait for the leaves to finally stop

dropping! I'd like to get this yard work done and the tools put away for the winter." Vanessa's cheeks, reddened from the physical work and a nip in the air, and the wind-woven curls that swept around her face and neck gave her a fresh, wholesome look. She looked around at the yard and sighed. Her son kept on raking, not looking up.

"So I see you bagged your deer," said Michael, trying out his newly acquired jargon.

The neighbour raised her eyebrows and hesitated for a moment. "Oh! Yes. We did. My husband shot it. Did you see him bring it in?" she asked quizzically.

"No, actually, we saw it hanging in carport from our living room window. Didn't mean to be voyeurs." Michael cleared his throat. He knew he had revealed too much about how little privacy their neighbours actually had. "It was hard to miss! Just hanging out, back there." He laughed awkwardly.

Vanessa forced a smile. "Oh. I see. Or I see you can see!" She said with a knowing smile while pointing one finger at Michael. Both Michael and Margo laughed and nodded.

"Margo noticed it first, didn't you hon." Michael nudged Margo with his shoulder.

Margo wanted to stomp on his foot to tell him to shut up and move on. Instead she looked down at the ground. "I did." Then she gave Michael a quick warning glare and turned to Vanessa and said with a smile, "I guess you'll be filling your freezer this winter." Vanessa smiled and nodded. "We certainly will. It's always a savings, with meat prices so high these days. And my husband loves to hunt."

"Good for you. Great to see younger people taking up the traditions of living off the land like their fathers, and their fathers before them," Michael replied.

"And mothers!" Margo added, her eyes cutting to Michael. "And you're doing such a nice job on your lawn, Vanessa. We will have get at it soon ourselves! Gotta keep up with the neighbours! Well, enjoy your day!" With that she hooked her arm into Michael's, indicating that she wanted to walk on.

"You too!" Vanessa replied, "Oh, Margo. I wanted to invite you to an event I'm having next Saturday afternoon. We will be making our own facial cream from botanical oils and vitamin E. We will be making it using the product line I represent. I made up a batch for my mom. I think she's about your age actually. You should see the difference in her skin since she started using it! So much more hydrated and younger looking. I hope you come and try it out. I'm positive after one month, you'll see real results. I'll also be introducing my line of antioxidant supplements to boost your immune system. You're not obligated to buy anything, of course. It would be a good way to get to know some of the other ladies in our community!"

Margo listened to Vanessa's spiel politely, and replied, "Thank you so much, Vanessa. I'll check to see what we're doing Saturday and if there isn't anything pressing, I'd love to drop by."

"Great!" Vanessa beamed. "Hope to see you then!"

Not if I can make up a pressing engagement first! Margo thought. During this brief encounter, Michael and Margo's dog, Chance, had disappeared around the corner of the house. Margo hadn't walked him on a leash much lately since Chance was friendly and so were the neighbours' dogs. She had forgotten he was with them until she heard a yip from somewhere behind the house. "Chance! Come! Here boy!" She looked around. No sight of him.

"Oh! No! I hope he didn't discover the deer!" Vanessa ran, with her rake in hand, towards the back of the house.

Michael ran after her and disappeared. Margo had no intention of following, preferring to wait on the front lawn. She heard Michael calling, "Chance! Drop it! Down! Give that back!"

Chance came running out from the backyard with Michael in hot pursuit. Firmly clenched between his jaws was a deer's leg, the hoof dangling from the ankle joint. Chance deked Vanessa and veered away from Michael who tried to tackle him. Margo didn't know if she wanted to laugh or scream. She wanted to laugh because the hoof bounced up and down from the ankle joint like a playful puppet, but she was grossed out about what Chance held so tenaciously in his mouth. Chance was having the time of his life.

"Chance! Stop. Sit. Drop it." Margo commanded. Chance obeyed each command in sequence and stopped, sat and dropped the leg precisely at Margo's feet. Michael and Vanessa stopped too. Isaiah had stopped raking and was laughing hysterically.

His mother put her hands on her hips, "Isaiah, please go pick that leg up and put it in the bin with the rest!" Dropping his rake, he sauntered over and picked up the deer leg while Chance watched with great interest, hoping the boy would throw it to him. He was disappointed when he saw Isaiah walk around the corner the house, bouncing the hoof from the ankle joint. Chance looked at the deer foot longingly, whining as his prize disappeared. He twisted around in his collar, but Margo wouldn't let him go until she had secured his leash. She knew she would have to drag Chance out of there and well down the road before she could trust him not to revisit the scene of the crime. Margo smiled at Vanessa and apologized for her dog's behaviour.

"Oh, no problem," Vanessa said, putting on a big smile. "Blake will dispose of the carcass when he comes home tonight. Meantime, I'll make sure that waste bin's lid is secured tight."

"Looks like no harm done anyway. Enjoy the rest of your day!" Michael said, recovering himself so Margo and Michael and Chance could continue their walk down their street. The sky was a blue dome above them. The maple trees were almost bare. The gold and red leaves that had fallen whirled across lawns and danced in the street as gusts of a cold north wind came off the mountain. Margo pulled her sweater closed. "It really is getting cool," she said to Michael. "Before you know it, we'll get our first snowfall."

Michael sighed. "Our first winter in our new home. I wonder what that will be like. I guess I had better get some firewood in. Ivan told me he would help me buck up the rounds he delivered."

"Listen to you! Talking about 'bucking up some rounds and bagging a deer.' Aren't you getting the hang of the local lingo! Next thing you know, you'll be dressing your own deer. Or should that be undressing your own deer?" Margo laughed at her own joke.

"Oh, no! Not this buckaroo!" Michael said jauntily. "There are some things I'd rather hear the old cowboy talk about on his porch than experience for myself."

The next morning, Margo woke up, surprisingly refreshed. The breeze coming through her open window was cool. Her nose felt cold but the rest of her body, underneath the covers, felt cozy and warm. She stretched and rolled out of bed.

Donning her usual morning lounge wear - loose fitting knit pants and an oversized sweatshirt, she made herself an espresso and settled down in her recliner to read the news on her phone and catch up with her friends' activities on Facebook. She thought she might even write a humorous story about seeing the dead dear hanging in the neighbour's carport. That ought to amuse or horrify her city friends - especially the animal lovers and anti-hunting activists. *Ah, retirement*, she thought. *What an adventure*! She smiled to herself at all the strangely amusing things she had encountered so far in this tiny community in the Kootenays.

With a sigh of contentment, Margo looked over the peaceful scene before her. The oversized windows in their living room where she could look over the roofs of the houses in front of them to the hills and sky beyond made it feel like she was viewing a scene of a charming village in a movie. Sipping her espresso, her eyes followed the path of the old man who stepped out of the house adjacent to theirs. He walked through the tall, unkempt grasses of their backyard, deliberately and slowly, with a bucket hanging from each arm. When he reached the fence line he stopped in front of the compost pile there. He set down the buckets, then picked up a smaller one already at the spot. He fished something out of the small bucket and dumped it into one of the larger buckets he had carried. The bucket seemed to emit a steam cloud when the object was dropped into it. Next, he turned over the bucket he had emptied and sat down on it. Leaning over the bucket he had just dropped in whatever it was, he plunged in one hand and pulled something out. Margo thought he might be washing and rinsing clothes or rags or something.

She took another sip of coffee and set it down beside her. *Whatever it was*, she thought, *it wasn't any of her concern*. She picked up her phone and was about to scan the news, but something she had seen caught her attention. After he had extracted whatever it was he had dropped into the bucket of hot water, he held it over the other bucket, pulling at something. Margo look up and stared.

"Wait! What?" she said incredulously and grabbed the binoculars. She focused in. "Is he plucking a chicken?"

CHAPTER ELEVEN

'Tis the Season: The Finer Points of Light Displays

On one of the first snowy days in December in their new home, Michael was staring out of the living room window at the snow-covered rooftops of the houses in front of him. They looked to him like a miniature village displayed in a store window. The scene before him prompted Michael to think about getting out his lights to decorate their new house. Without turning around, he called out to his wife, "Margo, can you remember where the boxes I packed with the outdoor Christmas lights ended up?"

Margo, too, was thinking of the Christmas season. She was looking out the kitchen window at the snow gently falling in slow swirling flakes and piling up into what looked like a soft white blanket on the street in front of her. Humming a Christmas tune, she was rinsing their coffee cups and plates and setting them in the drying rack. The new home, with a fire burning in the wood stove, felt warm and cozy and Margo was imagining how she wanted to decorate for Christmas. She thought for a minute about Michael's question and then turned towards him and replied, "I think they were stacked under the stairs. Pushed right to the back to make room for things we thought we would need before them. You'll have to take out all the other boxes and bins we stored under there to get at them."

Michael swiveled around in his chair and heaved himself out of his comfortable repose. "Well, they won't move themselves. No time like the present to get started!" Michael was always a doer, never a procrastinator. He liked to be active and relished a project to sink into since he had retired. Projects made him feel useful and gave him purpose. He still wasn't entirely comfortable with retirement and a blank schedule that he felt needed to fill each day.

Margo dried her hands on a towel. "I'll come with you." She followed Michael downstairs, and they began taking out the boxes and bins that had taken up the open space under the stairs.

"I thought we would get to organizing this stuff before now," Michael said.

"And I thought Christmas would never come," Margo replied dryly.

Michael burrowed further under the stairs, shoved each box forward and passed it on to Margo. After what seemed like it could be a hopeless mission to Margo, who was stacking one box after another in an orderly arrangement, Michael's muffled voice traveled out from under the stairs with good news.

"Looks like I struck gold! I found them. I'll pass

them to you one by one."

Margo's job was to extract the boxes Michael moved forward in a train that he pushed towards her through the tunnel he had made under the stairs."Last one!" Michael called, and then crawled backwards out of the crawl space.

Margo stacked the last box on top of the rest. "Twelve boxes," she counted. "All marked Christmas lights. Wow! I had no idea we collected so many lights. I guess we won't have to buy anymore this year! I think we have higher priorities than spending our pension income on Christmas lights."

Michael had extracted himself and arched his back to stretch it. Then he straightened up. He was looking at the labels on the boxes to make sure the inventory was correct. The labels all read 'Christmas lights' and they were divided into 'outdoor' and 'indoor'. Each label had the number it was of the whole collection so - 1 of 10, 2 of 10 and so on - so they could all be accounted for. Michael also kept a list of items they had packed to reference in case some went missing.

"There are ten boxes of outdoor lights and the equipment required to run them," Michael said, "and two boxes of indoor lights which you use to decorate your tree."

"Right." Margo stood up from where she had been crouching and stretched out her legs. "Let's get these upstairs! And then," she said, with excitement in her voice, "we can go out and get a tree!"

"First things first. Help me get these boxes upstairs and out onto the deck."

Margo followed Michael up the stairs with a large, lightweight box of light strings. Michael took the two smaller but heavier ones, with the equipment to run them. After six trips, all the boxes were upstairs and Margo was exhausted. "Getting old is not for the faint of heart!" Margo puffed up the stairs with the last box she would carry.

"Speak for yourself!" Michael was still running on adrenaline and eager to plan this year's light display. Just unravelling and laying the strings of lights out on the deck, end to end, took Michael half the day. The real work, though, would be designing the layout. He started by stringing lights along the eaves and down the sides to create an outline of the house. After linking up extension cords and strings, testing the light strings, and replacing bulbs that were breaking the circuits, Michael was ready to begin. Traditionally, Margo acted as Michael's assistant when he called on her to help string the lights. He liked to do the measuring, planning and layout himself first.

The two of them worked all afternoon to wind, staple, nail, and tie lights around the house and structures Michael had planned to light up. When they finished, Michael hauled two lawn chairs out of storage and faced them towards their house. He plugged in the lights and sat down with Margo to admire his handiwork. "Looks wonderful! Even better than last year's display!" Margo raised her cup of hot chocolate spiked with Baileys.

"I thought I would up my game this year because we are retired and I have the time and energy to devote to it." Michael raised his beer and clicked bottle to mug with Margo, then added, "Plus, we're in a new neighbourhood. First impressions are important."

Margo took a sip and glanced sideways at Michael. *First impressions, my ass*, she thought. *If this were a competition, he was playing to win.*

Strings of multi-coloured lights swirled down the posts rotating through red, blue, green, yellow. The addition this year was the freestanding nativity scene on the lawn that Michael had created out of lights and wire frames. Mary and Joseph were outlined blue. Baby Jesus in the manger glowed white. The outlines of the shepherds were green and red. A white and gold lit angel hovered over the scene - with the help of PVC pipe that supported it. And three wise men parked off to the left of the main scene were lit in gold, white and red.

"It's lovely, Michael. Really. But I wonder if it is too much. Look across the road. They don't have nearly the display we have." They studied the display.

Across the street, the neighbours with the precocious preschooler, had a string of multi-coloured lights swagged across their deck railing. In their front yard, stood a trio of plastic blow-up holiday figures - lit from the inside. Two snowmen, one listing to the left like it was already tipsy, stood on either side of a T-Rex dinosaur that had a present clamped between its teeth.

"Oh, I'm sure they will be fine," Michael said, dismissing Margo's concerns with a sweep of his hand. "Besides, it is early days yet. Maybe this display will prompt our neighbours to up their game."

Margo wondered if the neighbours would be wondering where they came from that they thought they should put on such an ostentatious show. Judging from the houses in the neighbourhood, this wasn't a 'keep up with the Jones' kind of community. In fact, it wasn't even a 'keep up' kind of place.

"Why don't we take a walk around the neighbourhood. It's a beautiful night," Margo suggested. Margo and Michael walked the two streets of their neighbourhood and the connecting streets. Margo took pictures with her phone of houses with light displays as they walked. There were a few decorated houses, but they weren't very sophisticated. Two houses had a single string of multi-coloured lights outlining the fascia. A door of another house was outlined in red and green lights. One unique display in a yard featured a unicorn lit up in white lights and a birdbath featuring a bare-breasted mermaid splashing in blue and white twinkling lights. Another had candy-cane shaped lights striped with red and white, strung along the wall beside the front door in a neat row.

When they came to Tina and Joel's house, they stopped. Tina and Joel were also new to the community, and also newly retired. Apparently, they didn't get the memo either that there was no competition. Their light display surpassed anything Michael had ever seen. The whole front of the house was strung with a grid of lights that were programmed to wave across the spectrum, lighting up in rotation so it looked like waves of white, then blue, then green, then red and then repeated. In addition, there was a lawn ornament that took the shape of a dolphin splashing into a waving pool of white, rolling lights.

As they were standing there, taking it all in, the

front curtain twitched. Tina waved from the window and gestured toward the door. She popped her head outside through the open door. "Hi ya!" Tina called out. "Looking at our light display? Joel and I just put it up. What do ya think?"

Michael didn't respond. Margo knew he was speechless because he was already comparing displays. "It's spectacular! I love the aquatic theme!" Margo was quick to fill in the gap.

"Yeah well, in LA, this kind of set-up with an ocean theme is very popular. We also decorate palm trees in California since we don't have evergreens. So we thought we would bring a little of our home to Wannatoka Springs. So? Whaddya think? Out of place here?"

Michael shook off his appraisal hat and added, "Why not! Dolphins rule!" He made an awkward raised fish punch, meant as a sign of solidarity and coolness.

"It really is different for us Canadians here in the great white north!" Margo giggled. "But I have to say, I think its grand! And around here, who tries to fit in anyway!" She smiled. "You and Joel should come over and see what Michael put together. It's a show stopper!"

"I wouldn't go that far," Michael demurred. "It's pretty traditional. But I had a good time putting it together."

"He's being modest. Its really is an amazing display, especially the Nativity scene outlined in lights. Michael is kind of a Christmas light virtuoso. He's like those pyrotechnics that design fireworks. Passionate about his craft and always wanting to make a bigger and better one next year."

"We'd love to stop by and see it," Tina said and then called inside for Joel. "Honey, Margo and Michael have stopped by to look at our lights. Do you want to walk back with them to see theirs?"

"Sure hon." Joel's voice carried over the muted voice of the hockey game announcer. Then he shouted, "Yes! Yes! And he scores!" to the TV.

"The Kings must've scored," Tina said to Margo and Michael. "I'll never be able to drag him away until after the game. Tell you what, how about we meet you there after it's over. We could be there in about an hour or so? Unless, of course, the game goes into overtime. In that case, Margo, I have your number. I'll text you."

"No, no, please don't change plans for this. How about we get together tomorrow." Michael suggested.

"Umm... Let me check my calendar. This is Wednesday, right?" Tina's eyes looked up and to the right for a second or two, "All clear from here to the weekend. Oh, yeah, we're retired, so it's all clear from here till the end of December!" She let a tinkling laugh escape.

Margo and Michael both smiled at the thought of their own clear schedules. "That would be lovely!" Margo pitched in. "I'll make us our special hot chocolate with Bailey's!"

"Great!" Tina said, "I'll bring my special cookies to go with your special hot chocolate!" They all laughed. But Michael was already wondering how he would turn them down or at least, only indulge in a bite to be polite. He didn't want to get as ripped as he was the last time.

Margo and Michael waved goodbye and sauntered down the street back to their house. "It is traditional," Margo said when she looked at it from the street, "But you did a really nice job of it. You should be proud of it!"

"It's OK, but did you see the flowing light show Joel set up? Ours just sits there. It doesn't move."

"How is it supposed to move? They are figures in the snow. I think they look regal," Margo offered.

"Never mind," Michael dismissed her response with a wave of his hand. "I don't expect you to appreciate the finer points of light displays, Margo."

Whenever Michael's tone was dismissive, Margo's 'sexist' alarm bells went off inside her head but she said nothing. Michael mounted the steps and opened the front door for Margo, she stepped inside. "You go on in. I'll be in a minute. I have something I want to adjust on my display."

Margo closed the door behind herself. *He's being furtive*, Margo thought. *And that means competitive.* Margo went downstairs to stoke the fire. She knew this wasn't over. When Michael became fixated on something there was no argument she could give to make him see sense. It was best to let him do what he was going to do.

On their walk back home, Michael had already been scheming about how to upgrade his light display. He thought he could attach a circuit switch to the lights so they blinked on and off in rotation so it looked like they were rolling. He had bought one last year. He hadn't thought he would use it this year because Margo mentioned that blinking lights annoyed her sense of peace at the time of year that was meant to be about peace. But hearing her gushing over Joel's sensational, over-the-top, rippling light display had made him a wee bit jealous of her admiration for another man's work.

After Margo went inside, he rummaged through the boxes of lights he had brought up from under the stairs. The circuit adapter must be in one of them. Success! He found the colour changing Christmas light adapter buried under strings of multi-coloured lights still in the box. He set up the box and plugged in the extension cord that led to the strings on the house and turned on the switch. The lights on the house rotated through a wave-like motion starting at one end, and snaking through to the other and back again in a perpetual wave. *That'll impress the surfer dude from LA*, Michael thought. But when he programmed the light strings on his Nativity scene, the wave action made him a bit seasick.

After a bit of experimentation, Michael thought he got it right. He connected strings of lights around individual shapes each into their own adapters and lit the whole display up.

"Michael," Margo came out, shivering in a throw she had wrapped around herself. "It's really late! And cold!" She stood shivering in the glow of doorway, wearing her sweatpants, an oversized sweatshirt and slippers - with a blanket draped around her shoulders.

Her silhouette reminded Michael of school plays where the Virgin Mary was dressed in a shawl, bending over the baby Jesus. He called out playfully. "Madonna! You have appeared to bless your humble servant!"

Margo laughed and picked up the narrative. "No, it is I. Your concerned wife. And I have appeared to tell you that you need to come in from the cold!" He hadn't even notice the cold, except for in his fingers when he had to take off his gloves to work on the connections. His adrenaline and excitement kept him warm.

"I believe I have done it, Margo!" Michael danced from one switch to the other, making sure the connection was secure. "I have set up a light display that will make Joel drool with envy."

"Is that so." Margo folded her arms in front of her, ready to challenge Michael's statement. "Let me take a look." She started to step out onto the deck, but just as she did, the display went dark.

"No, no. Not 'till tomorrow my love. But I promise you will be in awe!"

"Do you really think this necessary, Michael? I know you want to make a good impression, but why is it important that you make a bigger and better display than Joel's? Tina and I don't go around trying to make the best Christmas cookies!"

"You two wouldn't understand. Lighting is complex. Creating a lighting masterpiece requires ingenuity, logic and an understanding of technology. It's not just about lights. It's about demonstrating mastery. It's nothing like you girls baking pot cookies. That's a no brainer. Besides, It's a guy thing." Michael turned Margo around, playfully guiding her back into the house and shutting the door behind them.

Once inside, Margo turned to Michael to confront him. "I see, so us 'girls' - as you say - can't or won't become masters of lighting so we should stick with cookie baking and leave the heavy brain-lifting to you guys?" She leaned heavily on the words 'girls' and 'guys'.

"Exactly!" Michael said and gave her a peck on the cheek and a pat on her behind as he sidled by her.

He knew he was in trouble for saying that and wanted to escape to his man-cave. Margo swatted him playfully as he ducked under her arm and took the stairs down to his room. They knew each other well. Michael knew that referring to Margo, as a 'girl' would get her ire up. Margo knew that Michael knew that. So she didn't make a serious response. But she did let it smoulder. The taunt would ignite a future challenge.

The next morning, Michael went for a brisk walk, saying he had to get his legs un-cramped. He had been squatting in position for several hours the night before, setting and resetting his lights on the Nativity scene and then stretching up on his tiptoes on a ladder to reach the strings on the eves he had to change out. He went around the block and stopped in front his destination - Joel and Tina's house. Joel was out in his yard setting up yet another figure and lights.

"What are you setting up now Joel?" Michael asked.

"Oh, hi Michael," Joel looked up from his work, "I'm just adding to the west coast surfing theme. Tina found a Surfing Santa in my Christmas stuff we packed. Thought he ought to catch a wave on the snow."

The surfing Santa was a plastic blow-up figure of the jolly fellow, a red toque perched askew on his head, sporting white bushy eyebrows and a white beard swirling away from his face as if he was flying. He was dressed in a painted-on red, white and blue striped muscle shirt that stretched over his tubby tummy but didn't quite cover the space between it and the wild multi-coloured board shorts with palm trees printed on them. Surfing Santa was posed in a surfer stance with two pudgy knees bent, and his left arm straight out to his side to balance him. His right was holding a bag slung over his shoulder. Plastic presents popped out of the top of the bag. Joel had dug up and sculpted a slanted platform of packed snow underneath it. His sculptured drift had a curl at the top that hung over the body of it, making it look like Santa was had caught the big wave.

While the whole figure was a one-piece soft plastic inflatable figure, it was divided into several sections that were individually inflated and could be lit up in different colours from the inside. An electric pump was inflating Santa's body. As they talked, Santa started to stand erect on his surfboard.

"Wow! That's amazing," Michael said out loud, but in his inside voice he thought, *Dammit! How am I going top that*?

"You haven't seen anything yet," Joel said and pulled out his phone, trying out different effects. The surfing Santa stood on blue legs and became red in the face. Joel laughed. "A bit much maybe," and he toned it down with another touch. "I can also make it all one colour or no colour." The lights inside the plastic body glowed soft white through the colourful scheme painted on the outside.

"Tops anything else here in Wannatoka Springs!" Michael offered. "B.C. Hydro will sure love the Christmas bonus you will be giving them this year!" He studied the figure and the setting of the lights on the wall. It was daylight so none of them showed, but he could still see the display of dolphins splashing, waving lights in his mind's eye. And now, surfing Santa!

"I'm excited to see it lit up in the night! The kids around here will love it. A real novelty. Oh, just came to remind you that you and Tina are invited to come over this evening after dark sometime and enjoy a drink and a light up over at our house."

"Wouldn't miss it, neighbour!"

"Great! See you then." Michael continued his walk at an easy pace down Maple Street. When he turned the corner, out of Joel's sight-line, he started to run. He ran all the way back home and burst into the house and leaned up against the closed door, his chest heaving with the exertion.

Margo was baking shortbread cookies in the kitchen and humming a Christmas tune. She looked up, startled to see Michael in a state.

"Jogging now, Michael? The easy life of retirement must be getting to you."

"Gotta go to Crystal Lake, Margo, right now! Where are the keys to the car?"

"What? Now? What for? They're in the drawer in the buffet."

"Just something I forgot to get for tonight." Michael rummaged through the drawer until he found the keys, retrieved his wallet from the bedroom night table, and ran back out.

Strange, Margo thought to herself, *He didn't even take off his outdoor boots. That's not like him.* As soon as Michael was out the door, Margo picked up her phone and texted Tina.

Margo: Coffee cup emoji? Need 'girl' talk. Cookie emoji.

Tina: Sure! Coffee emoji. C'mon over.

Michael raced to the hardware store and found what he was desperately looking for in the Christmas decoration aisle. It was the last one. A Bluetooth remote control light show simulator that had eight different light programs: fade in, fade out, dragonfly, snowflake, pulse, alternate colour, wave, flash, and blink. It could also program the Christmas lights to pulse and change colour with the music playlist on your phone.

He sped home and went right to work. He made himself a sandwich and while he ate it, read the instructions and downloaded the app that controlled the remote Bluetooth adapter. When the adapter responded to the commands from his phone, he went outside to see how it worked.

The adapter was surprisingly easy to program. Michael credited that to the dumbing down of the next generation. Kids these days didn't have to learn how to do anything complicated, he thought. There was an app for that.

Michael experimented with configuring the lights with classic Christmas Carols and songs on his playlist. The lights shimmered and bounced with the beat of fast songs like "Sleigh Bells Ring," then slowly, solemnly faded from one colour to another when coordinated with classical carols like "Silent Night."

Michael was well pleased. But he thought one more item would top off the production - his stereo speakers. He went downstairs to retrieve them. Michael's speakers were relics of the 70s when he bought them to listen to rock music. The sound didn't warp at high levels and the woofers pulsed with a strong baseline. He could never trade them in for modern ones no matter how much other people bragged about their compact speakers with a precisely defined, concert sound that supported digitally recorded music better than vinyl on a turntable that mixed through amps.

Michael considered himself an audiophile and a purist. He still played records on a turntable through an amp where he adjusted the music tracks himself and listened to them through four-foot speakers that were perched on either side of his couch so he could listen to the stereo sound.

Michael brought one speaker up at a time and carefully set it down on the deck. Margo was reading in the living room and heard him going back and forth and inside and out, but decided not to interrupt him until she heard him stumble on the stairs.

"Need a hand?" She called out.

"No, I got this," Michael grunted.

The evening was drawing a shadowy curtain over Wannatoka Springs when Michael finished setting up his project outside. Margo and Michael ate silently, watching the six o'clock news and then washed up together.

After they had cleaned up, Michael went outside to make one last check on his light show. From her window in the kitchen, Margo could see the reflection twinkling in the gathering darkness. Margo had set out the hot chocolate mugs and was stirring the homemade hot chocolate in a pot when she heard footsteps coming up the walk - and voices belonging to her neighbours,

Tina and Joel, as they greeted Michael who was standing on the deck.

"Hi!" Tina said and hugged Michael. Her eyes were bright. Maybe a little artificially bright, Michael thought. Tina thrust a bag of cookies into Michael's chest. "My special cookies. To go with the special hot chocolate Margo is making."

"Oh, thank-you Tina! I'll give them to Margo." He opened the door. "Margo? Tina brought over her special cookies!"

"Thanks Tina!" Margo called over her shoulder through the open door. "I'll be out in a minute. Michael, just set them on the counter."

"I'll handle the cookies and hot chocolate," Margo instructed Michael. "You can get Tina and Joel settled outside and turn on the propane fire."

"Sure, hon," Michael said and went back out. "I've set up some chairs at the edge of the lawn along with a propane fire bowl. Thought we would be comfortable with some heat." Michael directed Joel and Tina to the chairs that faced the Nativity scene and the light display on the house. The lights on the Nativity scene were frozen. And the lights outlining the roof were slowly fading out and then fading in, in a different colour.

"Really nice setup!" Joel enthused.

"Love, love, love the traditional Nativity scene," Tina said. "You don't see that much anymore. I miss that from when we were kids. We always had a baby Jesus in the manger scene at home."

"We like tradition," Michael said. "But we also appreciate novel decorations too. Margo loves your dancing dolphin. And she hasn't even seen your surfing Santa display!"

Margo came out with a tray of steaming hot chocolate laced with Bailey's and caught the last couple of comments. "Yes! Your lights look spectacular, Joel! How did you get those lights on your wall to wave and change colour?"

"That's a highly guarded technical secret," Joel said in a confidential voice. "If I told you, I'd have to kill you." He winked at Margo took a cup of hot chocolate off the tray. "Just kidding, but it's complicated. Tina doesn't even know how to use the remote."

Tina and Margo caught each other's eye, smiled, and then quickly looked away, so as not to get the other one going.

"You should see the Santa on a surfboard Joel set up today," Tina said before Margo could respond with what she could tell was brewing in Margo's head right now. "He's wearing these spectacular board shorts," Tina smiled. "And, yes, Joel, I do know how to handle a plastic Santa. Just fill him up with hot air! Though I'm not as good as it as you are." She smiled again and took a sip of her coffee.

Margo giggled along with the joke.

"Women," Joel said with an exaggerated sigh, shaking his head.

"Can't live without 'em . . ." Michael responded.

"And ya can't kill 'em!" Joel finished. They clinked cups to cheers their shared understanding.

Tina and Margo looked at each other rolled their eyes. "Don't you just love Michael's display, Joel?" Tina said, changing the subject.

"Its great!"Joel offered enthusiastically and took a sip of his hot chocolate, "Amazing hot chocolate Margo. Love it!"

Michael was thinking about the timing of the special effects he had programmed. So far the Nativity scene and the lights around the house were subdued. Joel had been complimentary but didn't sound impressed - not nearly as impressed as Margo had been with Joel's display.

With a push of a button on his app, the light show should come to life with the first carol, "It Came Upon a Midnight Clear." He had programmed the lights on the house to slowly fade in and out to different colours and the Nativity scene to glow, first white, then blue, then green and red, blinking in an alternating sequence. After that song, he had planned a medley of traditional carols that would highlight the virgin birth and the manger. Michael wanted his display to differ from Joel's, not so much attention-seeking showmanship as classic sophistication. He was hoping the program would impress Joel and Tina, but especially Margo whose taste, he would describe as conservative and classic.

Margo had passed around her shortbreads and the special cookies Tina made. Michael made a show of biting into one and then pocketed the rest. Margo ate half of one too and left the other half on the plate - in case she wanted to indulge in the other half later in the evening. Margo and Michael had learned their lesson when Tina had brought over her sample and were consuming them in moderation. Tina and Joel ate one each with one without a thought. As they were talking, warming their hands on the portable propane fire Michael had set up, Margo felt the effects of the pot she ingested take a light hold on her - just enough to make her feel giddy. After a while, the men and women drifted into two separate conversations. The men were comparing techniques and programs they had used to set up their light shows. Tina and Margo were whispering and giggling, heads together conspiratorially. Time to start the show, Michael decided.

Michael rose from his seat. He had his cell phone in his hand and was thumbing through it. "Time to light it up!" he said excitedly and pointed the phone at the house where the programmable circuit adapter was plugged in. "I made a playlist of traditional Christmas songs starting with 'White Christmas'. Just sit back and enjoy the show folks."

The music and lights took on a life of their own. Instead of playing the subdued, sad sounds of the song he had chosen to start his show, Michael's speakers hammered out the first bars of "Rockin' Around the Christmas Tree". The lights danced around the Nativity scene while the lights outlining the house pulsed to the steady beat of the bass.

The once solid outlines of the shepherds broke into blinking red and green stripes, shimmying with a 'beep-beep' flash of green and then red solid lines. Mary and Joseph swirled in blue and white, taking turns to flash blue then white, in time to the music. The angel glowed white to brighter white then the lights circulated around the frame in a dizzying display hovering over the scene in iridescent splendour. The white and red lights of three wise men who stood off to the left, scattered like stars on the snow - like disco balls. Flashing stars and fireflies swirled around their luminescent crowns.

The baby Jesus who, up to this moment, lay passively in the manger outlined in white, revealed an alter ego. His arms and legs, composed of two strings of lights on wires, hidden until they lit up, flailed around in time to the music.

"W-o-o-h-o-o!" Tina shouted out. She jumped up from her seat and started dancing. Her eyes fixed on the display.

Michael stood, mesmerized, not trusting his eyes, since he had had half of one of Tina's pot cookies. He didn't dare ask if anyone else was seeing what he was seeing, in case he was hallucinating. If he was, he didn't want to admit it. He turned back to and Margo and whispered, "Is this for real?"

Margo beamed with delight. Leaning forward she said in a hoarse whisper, "Your eyes do not deceive you, my darling!"

Joel laughed out loud and stood up. He clapped Michael on the back. "You've done it, neighbour! You've pulled off the best light show of the season in Wannatoka Springs! Maybe in all of Canada. I just can't compete with that 'Great White North' spirit!" He couldn't help but start rocking to the beat of the rocking Jesus.

Margo stood and took Tina's outstretched hands, an invitation to dance. A rush came over her, and for a blissful moment, while she was rocking around with Tina, Margo felt like time had wound itself backward and she felt free like she hadn't felt since she was a child at Christmas.

Michael stared at his phone. He was still distracted by what had happened to his carefully designed program. But when he looked up and watched Margo and Tina let loose, he started to chuckle. This may not be his intended program, but it was fun! He found himself grinning and bobbing his head in time to the rockin' Christmas song. *Tradition is over-rated*, he thought, and tapped the camera app on his phone and held it up to capture the moment with a click and a flash.

Suddenly, the music abruptly stopped! And all the lights blinked out. The women were still singing "Rockin' Around the Christmas Tree". . . when they noticed there was no accompaniment and no lights to dance to. They were in the dark. Except for the light from the kitchen shining through the window.

"What the hell happened?" Joel did a three-sixty as if looking for some intruder who had snuck in and tampered with the system.

Michael found himself laughing at the sudden black out. "Sorry folks. I have no idea what's going on here, but, I'll see what I can do to fix it." He made his way to the deck, and turned on the outside lights to see what he was doing. "Meanwhile, maybe Margo, you could rustle up some more drinks?"

Margo sidled up to Michael and was peering down at the mess of extension cords Michael was attempting to untangle and follow to the adapter. "Sure I can't give you a hand?" she asked.

Michael held up a hand and waved her off. "Thanks for the offer but you wouldn't know where to start and I don't have time to explain it to you. Best we both stick to our separate spheres."

Margo frowned but held her tongue. "Aye! Aye! Mine sphere is to serve. I'll get right on that!"

Tina and Joel were looking on at the action, warming their hands on the propane fire bowl.

"Anything I can help you with, Michael?" Joel's voice rang out.

"I don't know. It may be a fuse. Or it may be a computer glitch. I'll take this down to my music room and see what I can do. If I'm not back in five, come get me. I don't want to spoil the atmosphere."

"I'll go down there with you," Joel offered and followed Michael into the house.

Tina followed Margo into the kitchen. She sat down on a counter stool and giggled. Margo grabbed a bottle of red wine from the wine rack. She poured Tina and herself a glass and held up her glass for a toast. The two clinked glasses and took a sip.

"Well, that was fun!" Margo said.

"Yup!" Tina smiled.

"Boys will be boys!"

"Yup!"

"You're a pretty good dancer, Tina."

"Thanks!" Tina laughed. "You aren't so bad yourself!"

Both women laughed and then clinked their glasses of wine in a silent toast to themselves. Coming from downstairs they heard the sombre tones of traditional Christmas music and the muted voices of the two men discussing possible reasons for the changes and trying out different settings on the app Michael had programmed.

"Think we should rescue them?" Margo asked.

"They're big boys. Let them rescue themselves." Tina waved dismissively. "I think we should have another glass of wine!" She held out her glass. Margo refilled both of their glasses.

Half an hour later, the two men emerged from their conference, shaking their heads. They were drinking beers that Michael had rooted from the fridge in his self-declared man-cave.

"Not a fuse. Not a computer glitch. The music on my phone runs as I programmed it," Michael said. "No idea what got into it. Gremlins, maybe? Anyway, I'll run it through tomorrow in the daylight. See if I can work the bugs out."

"It was great while it lasted!" Tina said enthusiastically.

"Good show, Michael!" chimed in Margo, lifting her glass. "And totally unexpected! Let's all raise a glass to the technical wizard in our midst - boldly going where no one in Wannatoka Springs has gone before!"

Everyone except Michael raised their glasses and said in unison, "Here! Here!" then took a sip of their beverage.

Michael frowned and rubbed the back of his neck in embarrassment. He mumbled, "I'll get to the bottom of this. You can bet on it."

"Meantime, let's just enjoy the night," Margo sipped her wine. "Oh look at that moon! I think it's almost full!" She was looking out the living room windows at the moon rise, scattering light on the snow.

"So bright! Who needs artificial lights," Tina concurred. "Let's all go outside and enjoy the light show in the sky."

Gathering around the propane fire bowl again, Margo snuggled into Michael and Tina held Joel's hand. All four sipped their beverages in silence, and looked at the outline of the Nativity scene before them casting soft shadows in the snow by the light of the moon.

After they said good night to Tina and Joel, Margo stood on the deck watching Michael turn off the propane and carefully take another look around to size up any danger that might be lurking.

Margo stopped Michael at the door and gave him a long, warm hug. "I love you, you know and I had a wonderful night despite everything not going altogether as you planned."

"Love you too," Michael hugged his wife back and said in her ear. "You were so much fun tonight. I think retirement is beginning to really look good on you."

Later that night, Tina texted Margo.
Tina: That was fun!
Margo: Right? Who said, "I don't expect you to appreciate the finer points of light displays." . . . oh yeah. . . Michael!
Tina: laugh/cry emoji
Margo: Know the set up tomorrow?
Tina: Hack Joel's phone and reprogram the app.
Margo: Thumbs up emoji.
Tina: What time you and Michael coming over?
Margo: Eight? Song?
Tina: Great! Eight it is. "So This Is Christmas". Santa deflates, dolphin goes dark and music slows to a stop.
Margo: Can't wait to see their reactions! Laugh/cry emoji
Tina: Women! Can't live with 'em. Eye roll emoji
Tina: And ya can't kill em! Laugh/cry emoji
Margo: Thumbs-up emoji C U @ 8!!! fireworks emoji

CHAPTER TWELVE

Margo and Michael's Christmas Tree Misadventure

For Margo and Michael, the community of Wannatoka Springs was the perfect place to retire. It was peaceful, quiet, friendly and virtually crime-free. But, like all idyllic communities there was always one neighbour whose habits and ways took getting used to.

In this neighbourhood it was Ivan Kantorovich. From one of the original families of Wannatoka Springs, he lived with his wife, across the road from Margo and Michael, in a farmhouse his grandfather built. It was one of the houses pulled up from the valley - when the valley was flooded to accommodate the hydroelectric dam located further south. The household consisted of Ivan, his wife Brittany, their precocious preschooler, Cassie. It was a rambling three-story house on three acres of land with plenty of room for all of them.

The covered porch where the family basically lived most of the year - smoking, talking, and sometimes yelling, was within earshot. Their voices were almost always pitched at a high volume as if one or more was hard of hearing. The conversations carried clearly across the street. None of them seemed to know or care that their neighbours could pick up every word of their personal conversations. The family also seemed oblivious to the colourful language they used when the family was outside on the porch. Margo, especially, felt uncomfortable to having to listen to them.

Even worse, were the exchanges between the parents and the precocious child. Their loud and insistently uttered demands would be met with a screaming tantrum if she didn't want to obey, which was most of the time. When it got too loud over there, Margo and Michael would give up their seats on their front porch and vacate to their backyard patio.

In the evening, the streets went silent in the village until Ivan started his stereo in his open garage and lifted weights to the pulsating sounds. When she heard the songs he chose start to spew out threats of corruption, destruction and death, Margo took that as her cue to go back inside and reposition herself as far away as she could.

Michael, who considered himself an audiophile, sometimes purposely went out onto their deck in the evening to listen to Ivan's playlist. He came inside one evening, to report to Margo that he recognized one of the bands blaring from the garage while Ivan powered up. The band was called Five Finger Death Punch. He thought he would look it up on his songs app.

One evening soon after his discovery of a musical connection with Ivan, Michael heard the song again coming from the garage. Michael headed across the street.

He stood in the shadows of the light coming from the garage for a moment, listening for a break in the songs and watching Ivan dead-lift three hundred pounds. He waited until Ivan had finished his reps and was toweling off his hands and face. Michael coughed to make Ivan aware of his presence before he shuffled out of the shadow, hands in pockets and said, "Hi there! I'm your new neighbour across the street, Michael."

Ivan looked surprised and then turned apologetic. "Sorry man, if this is about my f . . . n music, I'm OK with turning it down if it f . . .n bothers you."

"No, no," Michael waved off his concern. "Actually I came to tell you that I've been listening to it, and I think we have at least one group in common. I believe you were playing Five Finger Death Punch a song or two ago."

The comment caught Ivan off guard. He rose to his full height and, flexing his whole upper body, said, "What the f . . . does a guy like you know about Five Finger Death Punch?" He didn't sound angry. Just surprised. Surprised that a man as old as his own father knew anything about metal music - especially a man who obviously looked like an accountant or at least someone who didn't exactly dress the part for a head-banger.

"I listen to all sorts of music," Michael shrugged nonchalantly. As he said that, he widened his stance and crossed his arms across his chest in an un-conscious effort to look bigger and tougher. But if Ivan was a bear, Michael was a deer - and right now he was staring down the bear. Ivan moved towards Michael and stuck out his right hand. When Michael met his hand, Ivan clasped Michael's in his meaty grip, pulling Michael towards him as he did, and then clapped Michael on the back with hearty exclamation, "Glad you came over! You're f . . .n OK! I'm Ivan." Michael tried not to wince in Ivan's grip and extracted his hand as soon as he could. "You wanna f . . . n beer?"

"Oh no," Michael replied, "I didn't want to break up your work-out. Just wanted to introduce myself and tell you that I'm a fan of most of your music. Do you know the guy who built my house enclosed it with nine inch walls? I can't hear a thing from inside."

"Yeah, Leonard overbuilt a lot of things in that house. He was obsessed. But that's another f . . . n story. I'm pretty much wrapped up here, so why don't you stay. C'mon. I've got a f . . . n beer fridge in my f . . . n man-cave here." Ivan walked over to a smaller and older and grimier version of the modern fridge and opened the door with a jerk of the handle. It was fully stocked with one kind of beer. Apparently, the only kind Ivan drank was Canadian. Michael, being a craft beer man, rarely if ever (unless he had no choice) drank what he called the worst of Canadian culture. This was one of those occasions, however, where he made an exception.

"Love a cold one." Michael said, hoping he sounded like a guy who drank beer at any time of day. Ivan threw him a beer from the fridge, which Michael caught - after a slight fumble - and followed Ivan up to his porch.

"That was "Never Enough." It's on their *Decade of Destruction* album. I have it on my playlist," Michael said confidently. He didn't exactly tell a lie. He did recognize the band but he had to do a search on his music app find the song that had the lyrics he remembered - "In the end we're all just chalk lines on the concrete." When he found the song he downloaded it and then listened to the whole album. He did that just so he would have something in common with Ivan when he introduced himself. Michael often said that the best way to make friends was to find music in common.

The two men, one a burly thirty-four-year-old weight-lifter wearing a tight muscle shirt that showed off arms like tree-trunks and jeans that stretched taut over muscular thighs, and one sixty-five-year-old retired number cruncher wearing a golf shirt that hung loosely around his slim frame, paired with neatly pressed jeans, sat together on Ivan's porch staring out across the street at Michael and Margo's tidy little bungalow. As they drank their beer, they discussed the merits of their favourite metal bands. The conversation became more animated with each beer they consumed. Michael finally excused himself while he was still on good terms with Ivan. He knew he couldn't win the dispute about who were the best head-bangers of the 90s.

By Christmas time, the two men had formed a loose bond. Ivan offered to plow their parking spot on the street in front of the house and taught Michael the finer points of chopping wood. Margo didn't exactly bond with Ivan's wife, Brittany, but she did bring over chocolate chip cookies once in a while. When she saw Margo sitting on her deck as she drove to work, Brittany sometimes leaned out of her car window to ask if she needed anything from Crystal Lake. Margo waved back and thanked her, but always said she didn't need anything.

Cassie took a shine to Roscoe, Margo's cat, who

had claimed the swing on the deck as his territory. She crossed the street often and climbed up onto the deck whenever she thought she could get away with it. She could be found swinging with Roscoe while she patted him and talked to him. For some reason, the cat that put everyone else in their places including Chance, let this little girl pick him up and carry him around the yard like a dead weight, or tickle his ears with a blade of grass while he shook his head quickly to relieve the annoyance. He never clawed or bit her but drew the line at having his tail pulled. Fortunately Cassie was a quick learner and the first time Roscoe turned around and hissed, she backed off and never repeated the assault.

Margo didn't mind. It did give her an opportunity to connect with the family across the street when she heard them hollering for Cassie. When she heard Cassie's name being called, she would poke her head out the door and if she saw her on the swing, would talk her into going back home by telling her Roscoe was tired and needed a nap.

The holidays had always brought out the baker in Margo so she thought, this year, she would bake a batch of shortbread cookies, wrap them up in handcrafted decorated boxes she had learned to make watching a YouTube channel. Now that she had the time to devote to anything that took her fancy, Margo found she actually liked crafting. The problem was that the crafts she made didn't always work in their minimalist home. So, this Christmas she had the idea she would make decorative boxes and fill them with cookies to hand deliver to the neighbours. It was an old-fashioned idea, and she wasn't sure how she would be received, but she decided she would go through with it anyway.

The other thing about the Christmas season that Margo absolutely loved was bringing in a real tree they bought from a supermarket. This year, Margo was excited because they were living in an area surrounded by forest. She fantasized about going out with Michael into the snowy woods, choosing and cutting down their very own tree.

Margo grew up in a small town in northwestern B.C. and as part of the tradition, Margo's father would travel to a wooded area nearby and cut down a tree. Although Margo would have loved to have gone, he emphasized that this was a 'man's job' and that she should stay with her mother and fix up something warm for the men when they came back with a tree.

A traditional rural Canadian man of his generation, Margo's father separated tasks into female and male worlds. He wanted to bring up his son to excel in the 'manly arts' of chopping wood, building things and making fires. Little did he know then that her brother would have no use for those skills when he grew up. Upon graduation from high school Margo's brother followed his love of numbers, became a stockbroker and came out as a gay man. He lived in Vancouver's west end, in a condo tower that overlooked English Bay. He never did a day's work in his adult life that callused his hands or required the use of an axe or a flint. He started his BBQ on his deck with the push of a button and the only Christmas trees he decorated with his partner were artificial - usually in unrealistic colours like pink or silver.

Margo, however, caught the bug of pulling in a

real tree to decorate and filling her home with joy of sight, smell of the season. Everything had to be authentic - from the smells of shortbread with a pound of butter in each batch, to the soft instrumental Christmas music she set up on her own playlist, to the pungent perfume of pine or fir from a freshly cut tree decorated with sparkling lights and delicate decorations.

It was mid-December. Margo had made her gift boxes and packed them with shortbread, ready to distribute to the neighbours. She thought now was the time to spring her idea about cutting down their own tree on Michael.

One evening, while they were sitting in front of the wood stove enjoying the warmth and the mesmerizing glow of the flame, she turned to Michael.

"Michael, don't you think it's time to get our tree?"

Michael was lulled into complacency by this time, due to the two glasses of red wine he had consumed and the light of the fire. He just smiled and agreed. "Yes, now would be the perfect time."

Margo didn't respond, but let that idea settle in Michael's head. A beat later, Michael said, "Where would we get one, though? I didn't see any for sale in front of the hardware store or building supply in Crystal Lake when I cruised by last Saturday."

That was the springboard Margo was waiting for. "Of course not! That wouldn't be authentic. In rural B.C. people go out into the wood and chop down their own tree."

"Hmm. . . I never thought of that. I'm sure if I asked Ivan he would go out and chop one down for us when he goes out to forage for firewood to sell." Michael patted Margo's knee and then settled back into his chair and took another sip of his wine. Problem solved, he thought.

Margo was still working up to her idea. "That would be OK I guess, but I was thinking . . ."

"Always a dangerous proposition," Michael joked - but somewhere in the recess of his mind a red light started blinking. When Margo said those words, he would probably be drawn into a plan that complicated and possibly challenged his wellbeing.

"Seriously, Michael. Listen to my idea."

"OK, shoot. I'm listening." But Michael was still staring into the flames and letting his mind drift freely.

"What if . . . I mean we now live in a small village surrounded by forest - so it makes sense - what if we go out into the forest ourselves and cut down our own tree?"

Michael laughed. "Right. I can picture it now. The pair of us, a couple of retirees who have spent all their adult lives living in a city where trees are protected in parks, will become foresters and chop down our own Christmas tree." He grinned at the image that conjured up.

"You may have spent all your life in the city. But I grew up in a small town up north and my father went out every Christmas when we were kids to chop down a Christmas tree." Margo didn't say he only took her brother with him. That didn't matter. What mattered was that she knew it could be done. She could have done it, she figured, if her father didn't think it wasn't a 'girl's job'. To Michael she said, "C'mon. It would be an adventure. We could use the side-by. Wouldn't it be great to go out there and chop down our very own tree and bring it home? Think of how meaningful that would be for us, for our very first Christmas at Wannatoka Springs. Think of the stories we could share with our city friends!" Margo paused and let her words sink in. She knew, like a good salesperson, not to oversell and to stop talking after the pitch. She turned and watched the fire.

"I think you need a chainsaw to do that. I don't own one. And even if I owned one, I wouldn't know how to use it."

"But you know you've always wanted one," Margo cooed enticingly. "Remember this fall when all we could hear was the buzzing of chainsaws coming from across the road when Ivan was cutting logs into firewood size and how you went over there and to look at what he was doing? And remember how he came over and showed you how to split wood with a maul? You'd never used one of those before either."

"Yeah, but we're talking chainsaws here. They're heavy and unwieldy. Dangerous. Ivan's a big guy and he's fearless. He could wrestle a crocodile!"

"It's not about size. It's about technique," Margo said, looking at Michael with a sly smile. The innuendo was not lost on Michael who smiled back at Margo. "C'mon. It would be fun!" She continued her campaign. "Tramping around in the woods. Looking for the perfect tree. We could take Chance. He loves the snow. And I could pack a thermos of soup, and one of coffee - maybe even add some rum to warm our innards!" Margo shivered dramatically. "But not too much for the driver."

"Sure, I'll drink and we'll let Chance be our designated driver," Michael shot back.

Michael rose and fed the fire with another log.

He thought of how he had learned this summer to split rounds with a maul he bought at the hardware store. He bought the rounds from Ivan who was selling firewood. Ivan had taught him how to handle the maul so that the weight of it cleaved the wood on the downward swing. It had taken him half the summer and most of the fall to buck up all the wood and, at first, a lot of shoulder and elbow pain and chapped hands until his muscles and hands had hardened up and he got the hang of splitting and stacking.

In early November, Michael had posed at the woodshed proudly as Margo snapped a photo of him in front of an six-foot-high stack of split wood four layers deep. She had posted it on Facebook with the words, "My Woodsman". Margo was so proud of him. And he was proud of himself, that he could bring in a wheelbarrow full of wood to stoke the stove in the fire and take the chill out of the house.

Michael closed the door of the stove with an oven mitt protecting his hand. He stood up and flung the glove onto the wood stacked to one side and turned to face Margo. "Alright. I'm in. Let's go get our first Christmas tree."

Margo was elated. "What about the chainsaw? Do you think Ivan will lend out his?"

"No way. A guy doesn't lend out the tools he uses to make his living. Besides, I've had my eye on one in the hardware store. It's top of the line, a Stihl and it's on sale, fifty bucks off with a company rebate."

"You've been thinking of doing this all along, haven't you Michael!" Margo exclaimed.

"Honestly? The thought never crossed my mind. But I had been thinking a chainsaw would come in handy next year. I could cut up firewood and prune the plum trees and such. And what better excuse to buy one than to cut down a Christmas tree with my woman!"

Margo squealed with delight and almost toppled Michael backward into the hot stove when she spontaneously jumped up and embraced him. Michael righted himself and led them in a little happy dance around the floor. After they settled down, the two spent the remainder of the evening reminiscing and laughing about their retirement adventures so far and talking about how they were going to prepare for this next one.

A few days later, on a crispy cold, sunny day in December, Margo and Michael set out on their adventure to cut down a coniferous tree and bring it home to decorate for their first Christmas in Wannatoka Springs.

"Got the rope?" Michael called out to Margo.

"Got rope!" Margo called from when she and Chance were standing beside the ATV.

"Got the gloves?"

"Gloves. Check."

"Shovel?"

"Shovel. No. I don't see the shovel." Margo called back.

"OK I'll pick it up from the shed. And I'll bring the chainsaw."

Margo danced excitedly on the road beside the ATV parked in front of their house. Chance joined in the fun by tagging Margo on the sleeve. Margo pulled her arm away and scratched behind Chance's ears. His eyes followed Margo's every move. He was panting with anticipation. Margo leaned into the box behind the side-by to take inventory. A cooler with a thermos of 'special coffee', a blanket, a snack of hummus, corn chips and carrot sticks. And, a couple of dogie treats for Chance.

Michael came around the corner of the house with a chainsaw that had a twenty-four inch bar. It was the longest chainsaw they had, Michael said. He said the store clerk asked him if he had handled a saw that big. He told Margo he had said, "It's go big or go home! And I'm not going home without a Christmas tree for my wife." Then he had handed over his credit card. As he talked, Michael was loading the chainsaw onto the ATV and tying Chance into the back, when Ivan saw him and walked over.

"Woowee! That's one f . . . n big-ass chainsaw," Ivan said.

"Yup! Going to cut down a Christmas tree!" Michael replied, admiring the saw that was now care-fully laid in the back of the side-by. The look on his face, resembled a boy's admiring gaze at his first fish lying in the bottom of the boat.

"Sure, you can f . . . n handle 'er?" Ivan grinned at Michael. Margo had her misgivings too, but didn't want to undermine Michael's enthusiasm. After all, he had agreed to go out and cut down a tree with her.

"Oh, yah. I can handle her." Michael patted the chain saw that sat in the bed of the box. "Thanks for that lesson, " he said, and tipped his hat to Ivan. "I think we're good to go!"

"OK neighbour," Ivan pushed himself off the side of the ATV. "Go out, get yourself an f . . . n beauty. But be careful out there. It ain't a f . . . n shopping mall."

Michael nodded in affirmation and straddled the low side gate to ease himself into the driver's seat of the open side-by-side. Margo waved to Ivan as they pulled out and Chance barked twice, signaling that the adventure had begun. All three had big grins on their faces as they slowly climbed the road that led them to the bush. "No Major Tom in sight on the municipal road," they joked. Once on the logging road Ivan had described to him, Michael breathed out a big sigh of relief. He and Margo were actually doing this!

Today was going to be a spectacular day, Margo thought. She watched the sun play hide-and-seek through the tall timber that lined the road and the snow lay like a soft blanket in the shadowy woods. The ATV chugged slowly up the hill. Michael concentrated on steering. Chance turned his head into the wind. With ears pinned back, he sniffed the new, exciting smells from the surrounding woods.

When they had climbed to a plateau that Ivan told Michael about, Michael stopped the ATV so they could survey the territory. Margo unhitched her seatbelt and jumped out first. Michael put the vehicle into park a before he disembarked. With a bit of a struggle, working against a dog eagerly struggling to be free, Margo unfastened Chance's rope. Chance bounded out of the vehicle and ran circles around it, abandoned to his doggy glee. Then he ran straight into the woods.

"Dammit!" Michael stood watching Chance disappear into a copse of trees. "We'll never get him back."

"Don't worry about it for now. Let him run. Where can he go?"

"I guess. He'll come back when he's tired. Let's get this show on the road!"

Michael turned slowly in a circle taking in the landscape. The area had been logged so it was more open than the dense wood they had come through. Ivan had recommended it because there would be some new growth they could access more easily. The scene looked nothing like what Margo imagined. She had always imagined a logged forest to be smooth and grassy, with the odd stump here and there, cleanly cut at about a foot off the forest floor. The scene before her was a debris-littered, denuded landscape with snow covering the worst of it, making it dangerous to walk on since branches and split trunks of dead trees stuck helter-skelter through the brush that was growing up around and through it. Here and there were spindly fir saplings, weakly stretching up above the snow-covered debris. Some were over eight feet tall, but most were between four and six feet. Margo wanted to cry. This wasn't what she envisioned when she thought of going into a forest to chop down a tree.

She had imagined a forest full of trees with a cheerful blanket of snow covering their feet, and hearing the faint sound of horses hooves and the jingling of bells in the distance. Waking herself up from her fairy tale, Margo said, "I don't think it would be fair to take any of these trees down, Michael. Look how hard they have struggled to reach the sky through this . . . this lunar landscape!"

Michael stood by Margo and looked on, too. He

was thinking about how hard it would be to climb over the debris and make his way with a chainsaw to skim off a tree and then haul it back to the ATV through the brush. He was secretly glad that Margo felt sorry for the trees. It gave him an excuse to move on to hunt easier prey.

"You're right, Margo. They do look like they deserve a chance. Besides, it doesn't feel right to cut down a tree that other hands have planted. Let's move on and explore the upper part of this trail. There must be trees that are still growing in their natural state. Even if we have cut down the top of one, it would be better and fuller than any of these poor specimens."

Margo agreed. She whistled for Chance. It took a couple whistles, but Chance finally came loping back through the thicket, a big grin on his face.

Traveling along the rutted, sometimes snow covered logging road, Michael kept watch for a reasonable size tree close to the road. He didn't want to have to haul one out of the bush if he didn't have to. He appreciated Margo's enthusiasm, but he didn't think she was strong enough and her help would be minimal. And, as for Chance, he would be useless - except as a cheerleader.

Up ahead Michael thought he spotted the perfect tree. It stood somewhat apart from the trees around it. About thirty feet high, it was straight and its branches tapered in an almost perfect conical shape to the crown. Michael stopped the ATV.

"There!" he pointed ahead and to the left of them. "See that tree standing all by itself? I think that's our tree."

Margo shaded her eyes and looked at the tree.

"It's a beauty! But isn't it a bit big? It will never fit in our house, even with the vaulted ceiling."

Michael smiled at Margo. Here was his chance to show off what a knowledgeable woodsman he had become - or thought he had become, having watched YouTube videos that taught how to correctly fall a tree, and what to look for in a tree you were going to cut down to size.

"You don't take down the whole tree. You just take down the top six feet or so. It's called 'topping a tree'."

"Oh. So how do you do that? We didn't bring a ladder."

"Stick with me, I'll show you how it's done. Let Chance loose and the two of you can walk up the road to the tree. I'm going to park this thing closer." Margo walked on ahead while Chance followed Michael in the ATV, barking as he ran.

Michael parked the ATV to one side of the road and then got out and walked around to the bed in the back. He leaned in and came out with the coil of thick rope he had packed.

"OK, Margo. I'm going to show you a little trick I learned watching a YouTube video on falling a tree. It's guaranteed to be safe. It'll work like a charm."

Margo followed Michael off the road, stumbling once on a branch or rock that was hidden by the ankle deep snow they were hiking through. She was glad she wore her almost knee high Sorrell winter boots she bought that winter. So far, she hadn't had any use for them, with the weather being mild and the snow not sticking in the lower elevations where they lived, but they seemed perfect for stomping around in the woods. She was equally glad for the down-filled parka she had also invested in. Winters in the lower mainland were mild and rainy. She would never have worn real winter clothes there, but she had purchased them hoping that the weather in the Kootenays was more like she had experienced in her childhood up north. So far she had been disappointed in the mild winter, but this trip into the woods renewed her hope in finding the magic once again in a winter wonderland.

When Margo stopped in front of the tree, she looked around. A pristine coniferous forest was all she could see. Tall, straight, trees cast shadows onto the snow. Patches of white between trees sparkled in the intermittent sunshine. And the smell of evergreen scented the air. Now this, Margo thought, was more like it. She was at home again, tramping around the woods with her father, the couple of times he allowed her to go with him when he figured she was old enough not to be a nuisance and sturdy enough to make her own way through the woods. Being in the woods brought back the memories of how much she loved the silence, broken only by her footfalls. The familiar giants surrounding her made her feel at peace. The only movement was far above them. A slight wind had picked up and the tops of the trees swayed as it ran through them.

Michael had managed to wrap the rope around a tree about sixteen feet away from the tree he had targeted and was tying a firm knot.

"Hey!" Margo called. "That's not our tree! What are you doing?" She struggled through the snow, making slow progress towards him.

"You'll see what I'm doing in a minute. First I have to secure this rope to this tree. Pick up the end of the rope over there." Michael gestured to the end of the rope lying in the snow. Margo fidgeted for her gloves in her pockets and put them on. She wondered if she shouldn't have brought work gloves. The leather gloves were not her best ones, but they were good gloves nonetheless and she didn't want to get them dirty or torn. Too late. She was here, and this was what she had. She grabbed the end of the rope and waited for Michael's next instructions.

Margo could hear Chance close by somewhere in the woods, barking. A split-second vision appeared to her - Chance was barking and running this way, bringing back some wild and dangerous animal that was chasing him.

"Got it?" Michael asked.

"Got it! Now what?"

"Walk it back to the tree we want to take down. Be careful. There are hidden branches and brush under-neath your feet. You don't want to twist an ankle."

"OK" she called back and picked her way care-fully through the underbrush, slowly advancing on the tree. Once there, she stood under it and turned around. Michael had gone back to the ATV and was coming towards her with his chainsaw. "Now what do I do?"

"Just stand there and wait for me." Michael retraced his steps slowly and carefully finding purchase as he advanced, carrying the chainsaw. He laid the chainsaw beside the tree. Putting his hands on his knees, he let out a long breath. "Made it!"

"Perilous trip! Glad you didn't fall!" Margo teased.

Michael straightened up. "I'm fine. Now, give me the rope. I'll take it from here."

Margo handed Michael the rope and stepped back about five feet to watch what Michael would do. She was surprised to see him set his feet and hands around the trunk of the tree with the rope looped around his neck and shoulders then shinny up the trunk of the tree. Margo had never witnessed such an acrobatic move from Michael. He was athletic. He had always played hockey and golf, but she never imagined him climbing a tree.

"Careful!" she called out.

"Don't worry," Michael grunted and shifted his weight from side to side, digging in with his feet when his boots found purchase and hoisting himself up one leg at a time. The lower part of the tree trunk was bare of branches. Michael had to climb about eight feet before he reached the first set of limbs. Reaching and turning, he pulled himself up and slung a leg over one of the branches then straddled it, facing the trunk. He waved down at Margo and gave her a 'thumbs up' with his gloved hand.

Margo stood tentatively - hoping against hope he wouldn't fall, and, at the same time in awe of the skills he was demonstrating. Right now she didn't know whether she was going to burst with pride - or throw up from anxiety.

Michael took the rope in one hand and felt around the tree, then completed the circle with his other hand. He jerked and dragged the end of the rope with his left, and let his right hand feed out the slack until the two lengths met. After that, he tied a sturdy knot to secure the rope around the tree. When he tested it by leaning his weight away from it - and frightening Margo with the daring aerial trick, he bounced back down the tree using the rope, hand over hand, to repel. He landed with a thump.

Chance was sitting, watching him the whole time. When Michael landed, he rushed over and licked his face, wagging his tail with relief that Michael was not hurt.

"Get off me! You know I hate it when you lick my face!" Michael pushed Chance away, but ruffled his neck affectionately.

"Amazing!" Margo said. "How'd you learn to do that?"

"Oh, I have skills you don't even know about." Michael smiled mischievously, standing up to brush off the snow. "Summer camp. My parents made me go every summer. Thought it would be good for a city kid to learn some survival skills in the woods - just in case."

"In case of what? You got lost in Stanley Park and had to spend the night and you had to build a signal fire to fend off wild squirrels while you waited for rescue?"

"Ha. Ha." Michael looked at Margo with a sarcastic grin and rubbed his gloved hands together. "Now, for the fun part. Here's where I need your help."

Michael walked to the other tree where the rope was tied to the trunk about two feet off the ground. He tested the sturdiness of the knot by leaning back against it. When he was satisfied, he called Margo over. He put a rope in her palm and wrapped her hand around it. "You're going to hold it steady just like this. OK?"

"OK," Margo echoed hesitantly, but wasn't sure

she was OK at all.

Michael continued with the instructions. "I'm going to go to our tree and use the chainsaw to cut it down. The rope will guide it so it will not go the wrong way, OK?"

"OK." Margo was sure now she wasn't. But she was the one who wanted to cut down a tree in the woods, and she'd be damned if she was going to back down now.

"Now, when I get about half way through the trunk, I'm going to holler at you to put your weight on this rope. Just hang off it. Bend your knees and lean back and just hang there. OK?"

"Seriously? You're going to use my weight to make the tree fall towards me?"

"It's OK. At first it will bend towards you. But when I tell you to, you're going to jump as far away as you can from the path of the tree. OK?"

"Stop saying OK! I'm not OK! This is not OK!" Margo stomped her feet and rubbed her hands together. Her hands were freezing and her feet were getting numb inside her boots.

Michael stopped what he was doing and looked Margo straight in the eye. "Do you trust me Margo?"

"Yes. I guess I do." She nodded slowly but was still suspicious about the plan and if she should trust Michael (who had never tried this experiment before) with her life.

"In all these years we've been together, have I ever put you in danger or tried to kill you?"

"No, not intentionally. I mean no." She shook her head emphatically.

"OK then. Just do what I ask and jump when I say. No one will get hurt. Then he looked around him at Chance who was lying in the snow chewing on a branch close by. He called Chance to come to him and to sit behind him so he would be out of the way. Chance obeyed for once. "I'll make sure Chance is behind me. Ready?"

"No?" Margo whimpered quietly, but then in a bolder voice said, "Ready." Then she stiffened her grip on the rope and clenched her teeth as she held on tightly to the slack rope.

Michael made his way back to the other tree, picked up the chainsaw, and revved it up in one draw of the pull cord.

Margo felt the vibration of the chainsaw biting into the wood and saw Michael leaning over it on one side of the tree holding it perpendicular to the trunk he was cutting into on the opposite side.

Suddenly, out of nowhere, a gust of wind whistled through the tops of the trees. The top of the tree Michael was cutting into at the base began to bend over towards Michael's side. The wind blew stronger. Margo looked up and saw the canopy of treetops bend like a choir bowing in unison for their encore. The trunk of the tree Michael was cutting swayed heavily towards him. The rope she was holding tightened. Margo hung on to it. Michael had told her to hang on. And hang on she would. Before she realized it, she was airborne. When she looked down, she saw that her feet were three feet off ground and rising. Having abandoned his chainsaw, Michael stumbled towards her over the uneven ground, flailing his arms in the air.

"Margo! Jump!" Michael called urgently. "Jump now!"

Margo felt her throat close up. Below her, the ground was swelling and receding. Her body was swaying with the tree like a piece of laundry flapping on the line. No way she was going to jump. She could see herself crashing into the brush below.

"Jump!" Michael yelled again. He was closer now, almost underneath her, with his arms reaching up to her feet. "I got you!" He could just touch her toes, but then the tree dipped the opposite way and the rope grew taut. Margo's toes lifted out of his grasp and he let go.

"Margo, you have to jump! I can't pull you down! When I say 'jump', just go for it! OK?"

"OK," Margo said, in a strangled voice. She was hardly able to speak. She felt the rope slack off and her body getting closer to the earth as the tree swayed towards the ground she was hovering over.

"OK! Now! Jump!" Michael called out. Chance barked in support.

Closing her eyes, and holding her breath, Margo let go of the rope. She felt the sudden shock of the ground on her feet that sent splints of pain up to her knees just before she fell back onto Michael who tumbled underneath the weight of her body. The two of them lay there for a moment, just breathing. They were both breathing, Margo realized. That was a good sign.

Michael struggled up first, gently rolling Margo off him. "I'm so sorry, Margo. That wasn't the plan. That wind came out of nowhere. The rope was supposed to stay slack. You were supposed to make it go lower, not let it take you higher. I'm so sorry! You OK?" He asked, smoothing her hair, now clotted with snow from the landing.

"Stop asking me that, Michael! I'm OK and I'm not OK. But I'm still here aren't I?" Then Margo started to laugh. Her laughter was contagious. Michael caught the bug and started laughing with her, mostly in relief that he hadn't killed his wife. Chance ran circles around the two of them, barking enthusiastically.

"That must have looked so funny seeing an old—er woman dangling from a rope in the woods while her man tries to cut down the tree it's attached to with a chain-saw. And then the tree lashes backward and up she goes up like she's in an elevator. Why didn't I turn on my video camera on my phone! This could have gone viral!"

Michael stood up, still laughing. "That's all we need. Our neighbours catching us doing something worthy of a Darwinian Award." He held one hand out for Margo, to help her up. Margo hoisted herself, and brushed off the snow, still giggling at the scene that kept running through her mind.

"Margo," Michael held up his hand. "I hear something. Shhhh. . ."

Margo stopped. At first she could only hear the wind's whistle through the trees. Then she heard it too. A low, steady sound - thump, thump, thump. Too rhythmic to be the wind. It seemed to be coming closer.

"Music?" She queried. "What do you think that is, Michael?"

"Metallica," Michael said, after listening for a while. "I recognize the band."

"Who? Metal - what? Listen. . . I think I hear a

motor running too."

The motor cut out suddenly, but the music still blared, crashing through the silence of the woods. Chance barked twice and ran towards the sound.

"Chance! No!" Margo called out, but Chance had disappeared through the woods in the direction of the cacophony. Presently, a man who cast a large shadow came tramping towards them. Chance was dancing proudly around him, as if he had found their rescuer.

"You f . . . n guys OK?" he called out.

Michael let out a loud whoop! "Yeah! Over here Ivan!

We're OK!" He looked at Margo and grinned. "It's Ivan!"

Margo couldn't help but roll her eyes, 'Well, they say God works in mysterious ways."

When Ivan reached them, Michael greeted him with a firm smack on his upper arm. Hey Bud, what're you f . . . n doing here?"

The hit didn't even make Ivan flinch. He looked like Paul Bunyan in his army-green hunting vest and his bulging arms encased in the red and black plaid wool jacket he wore under it. "I came out to get a load of f . . . n wood. Recognized your f . . . n side-by there on the f . . . n side of the road and thought I should see what kind of f . . . n trouble two f . . . n city seniors could get up to out here."

Ivan walked as he talked, spitting out f-bombs as if he was spitting sunflower seeds through his teeth. He went around the tree and followed the rope to the other tree. "What the f . . . did you think you were playin' at Michael?"

"I was using a technique I watched on YouTube. See the rope is supposed to guide the tree . . . " Michael started to explain the physics to Ivan, but Ivan just grunted, spat a gob of chewing tobacco on the ground and shook his head.

"You have no f . . . n idea. You could've f . . .n killed yourself," he said, and picked up the chainsaw and directed Michael to take the rope off. He told them to stand well back of the path of the tree. "Can't never tell 'xactly which f . . . n way a tree's gonna fall," he said. With a steady hand on the chainsaw, Ivan cut through the trunk halfway and then made a wedge cut downward to meet it. The tree swayed and they heard a loud crack.

"Timber!" Ivan called, and stepped backward with the chainsaw, shading his eyes while he looked up at the tree. It fell just beside the tree the rope was attached to, narrowly missing it and thus, saving the crown from damage. Ivan made short order of slicing through the treetop at the length Margo showed him. Then he wrapped the rope around the base of the cut, knotted it securely.

"How can I help?" Michael stood by Ivan watching him tackling the tree and trussing it up like a pro.

"Leave this to me. You go on up to your f . . . n ATV and be ready to haul her in," Ivan said. He shouldered the trussed up tree with a grunt and carried it up the incline to the road where the side-by and his truck were parked. Michael admired how his muscled arms easily swung the tree up off his broad shoulders and dumped it gently into the bed of his ATV.

"Ok, Michael, now I could use your help," Ivan said, brushing off his gloves.

"Sure, what can I do?"

"Catch the end of this f . . . n rope. We're going to cinch up this f . . . n tree."

Together the two men tied down the tree while Margo and Chance looked on. When they were finished Michael said, "Thanks, Ivan. I have no idea what we would've done without you here. Really appreciate it buddy."

"Probably f . . . n killed yourself! Don't worry, though, I would've come by sooner or later to pick up the f . . . n bodies." He winked at Margo. She grimaced at the thought. Chance was sitting beside Ivan panting. His eyes looked like he was gazing at his new hero. Ivan gave him a scratch behind the ear. "Chance here, would've survived. Smart dogs don't take f . . . n chances. And neither should you. I told you to stay in that f . . . n clear-cut for a reason."

His bravado having withered, and his ego deflated like a slow-leak in a balloon, Michael humbly shook Ivan's hand. "Well, we really appreciate your rescuing us, Ivan. Can we pay you for your work?"

Ivan looked offended. "Hell, no," he said and waved his hand dismissively. "I'll come back and harvest the rest of the f . . . n wood from the tree you cut down though. You OK taking it home?" He patted the box of the side-by-side.

"Sure, we're OK," said Michael. Margo looked at him and frowned. She wasn't sure she was OK.

Chance rode in the back with the tree, his legs enmeshed in its branches. You'd think he was the king of the forest the way he stood tall all the way down the road back to their home. Michael's pride seemed to swell up again as he passed a neighbour who waved at them and gave them the thumbs up.

When he saw Joel walking ahead of them, he slowed down and pulled up beside him. Joel looked up surprised, but when he recognized Michael he looked in at what he was carrying.

"See you got your tree!" Joel said as Michael slowed down to show it off.

"Yup!" Michael looked back at the tree, trussed up like a kill a hunter might bring home. "Just cut it down."

"Looks like a beauty!" Chance thumped his tail as Joel leaned in to admire the tree.

Margo beamed. "It's our first. I have always wanted to cut down our own tree for Christmas!" Michael sat taller in his seat the rest of the way home.

The next evening, Michael strung the lights around the tree. It stood in its place in front of their living room windows, winking at the neighbouring houses below them. Margo had dug into their storage and found the boxes of decorations she had packed and stored. But before she started the decoration, she wanted to set the mood. She lit the cinnamon-scented Christmas candles she found wrapped in one of the boxes, then whipped up spiced rum eggnogs for herself and Michael and set them on the coffee table. After that, she sat down on the couch wanting a moment to take it all in. The Christmas lights and fragrant scents brought back nostalgic thoughts about Christmases past. Margo took a sip of her eggnog and was about to begin unwrapping the ornaments when she remembered the Christmas music. That's what was missing! She thumbed through her phone's music library until she came to her favourite Christmas music playlist.

But before she could hit play, the music (if you could call it that) hit her full force. Screams wailed and bass notes thumped and vibrated right through the floor. Margo stiffened. What on earth . . .? Michael turned from his seat where he was admiring his handiwork and quietly taking in the scene.

"Let me guess," Margo said, "Five Finger Death Punch?"

Michael pushed his recliner down, and rose out of his chair. He walked toward the sound coming from outside the front door. When he opened it, there was Ivan, standing on the deck with a huge boom box on his shoulder, and a big grin on his face.

"Merry Christmas, neighbour!"he shouted. Then he turned down the music a notch. Margo could still hear it but it wasn't as assaulting to her ears. She crossed the room and stood beside Michael.

"Merry Christmas, Ivan!" she said.

"Thought I'd come over to see how the f . . . n tree wrestling went," Ivan said, and grinned.

"Oh it went great after we wrestled it into the house and stood it up." Michael opened the door wide so Ivan could see it. "Want to come in?"

"Oh, no, didn't mean to disturb you two. Just wanted to come over and give you this." Ivan handed Michael a thumb-drive. "It's got a lot of the music you said you liked on it. Five Finger Death Punch, *Disturbed,* Metallica. Thought you'd like it. So, there you go -

Merry F . . . n Christmas!"

"Oh! Thanks!" Michael said, and looked at Margo not sure what to say next. He hadn't even thought about getting anything for the neighbours for Christmas.

"Thanks, Ivan." Margo moved to the kitchen counter where all of the boxes of shortbread cookies were lined up waiting to be delivered to the neighbours. "I was just going to bring this over." Margo handed Ivan a delicately decorated box that looked as foreign in the giant hands as the present in the T-Rex's mouth on Ivan's lawn. "Shortbread cookies. They're my favourite Christmas cookies. I thought your family would enjoy them too. Merry Christmas to you and to Brittany and Cassie."

Ivan left soon after, turning up his boom-box and walking back with it across the street, one hand balancing it on his shoulder and the other carrying a daintily hand-decorated box of Christmas shortbread.

Margo leaned on the open door for a moment, watching Ivan walk up his driveway and listening to the refrain, "We're all just chalk marks on the pavement". She saluted the air with her cup of eggnog, repeating the refrain, "We're all just chalk marks on the pavement," unconscious that her foot was keeping time to the beat of the bass reverberating through the air.

"And a Merry Christmas to all, and to all a good night!" Margo announced, as she shut the door, accidentally leaning on the doorbell. "Damn!"

Author's Note

Thank you for reading the stories in **The Margo Chronicles**. I had so much fun writing them, I didn't stop at twelve. It's like the dilemma when I eat cereal with milk. When I get to the end of the bowl, I almost always end up with too much milk, so I add cereal. Then I have too much cereal for the milk so I add more milk - and so it goes until I have to say, "I'm full!" and push the bowl away. The stories I wrote for **The Margo Chronicles** have overflowed the number of pages I decided I wanted to publish as a book; I have five stories left over. So I decided to use them to start another book! I'm calling it **The Margo Chronicles Too!**

The stories in **The Margo Chronicles Too!** will pick up where Margo and Michael's first year of retirement left off - in the New Year. You'll recognize some of the familiar neighbours of Wannatoka Springs as you walk with Margo or ride with Michael in his side-by around the block from Spruce to Maple Street. And you'll be introduced to a few new quirky characters. Of course, Margo and Michael will find themselves in situations they aren't quite sure how to handle in the remote Kootenay community of Wannatoka Springs. So they 'll learn more about themselves as they roll with the adventure they have set out on - called retirement.

She Won't Last the Night

February in Wannatoka Springs meant that most of the residents went into hibernation. The ATV commuters took shelter, their ATVs put away for the winter. Only the hardiest, the dog walkers and the three older women who walked and together every day clutching walking sticks, could be seen walking on the icy roads. Although the winters were mild compared to other parts of the country, and downright balmy by prairie standards, most people preferred to spend their time around their warm wood stoves.

After their first summer and fall of meeting cordial neighbours who stopped on their walks to introduce themselves and exchange a few words, Margo was feeling confined and restless. She resorted to Facebook to feed her need for social interaction during the doldrums of winter. She commiserated with friends who were also feeling isolated and cold or envying friends who managed to escape the winter, travelling to the warmer climates. Shortly after they had arrived, Margo joined the Wannatoka Times Facebook page to keep informed about was going on in the community.

These days it had become her habit to peruse the community page, as she sat in the comfort of her living room recliner. She was hoping for something, anything. But there had been no social events planned since the social calendar was wiped clean by the sweeping social rules put in place to help curb the spread of the COVID pandemic. Most of the notices were posted by individuals looking for a ride to Crystal Lake, asking if anyone had seen their cat, or advertising eggs or homemade baking they were selling. On this February morning, Margo was scrolling through the *Wannatoka Time*s when she read an urgent message:

"HELP! PLEASE! My two year-old parrot escaped from my garage this morning. She was last seen around the motel. Her name is Precious. If you see her, please call or PM Birdie McLaren. SHE WON'T LAST THE NIGHT!!!"

Like *The Margo Chronicles?*
Post your comments!
Recommend it to the world online!

A new author, and a new book series, depends a lot on online recommendations to get launched and spread the word. If you liked **The Margo Chronicles**, I would really appreciate it if you wrote a review on Amazon and Goodreads so others can find it and enjoy it too.

Since I know you are already a fan, **I invite you to like and join the FaceBook page: *The Margo Chronicles* Author Page.** There you can comment and interact with me and posts by other Margo fans about the misadventures or characters in the stories. You'll also find updates on the upcoming publication of the next book in the series, dates and places where I will be presenting readings in case you want to come to one. I'll also be taking requests for readings - have story will travel.

Lightning Source UK Ltd.
Milton Keynes UK
UKHW020132081222
413524UK00013B/2037